T0159422

Murderesses
Two Italian Stories

Daniela Di Benedetto

Translated by Elizabeth Fraser

Trinacria Editions
New York

Translation by Elizabeth Fraser.

Published by Trinacria Editions, New York.

This compilation was first published in Italian in 2013 as *Chi Le Tocca Muore* by Officina Trinacria, Palermo, Italy. In the compilation, "Two Boyfriends Too Many" was originally titled *Due Fidanzati di Troppo*. "The Price of Revenge" was titled *Il Prezzo della Vendetta*.

Cover design by Louis Mendola. Photograph by Oksana Mitiukhina; used by permission (under license) from Shutterstock Ltd.

Printed in the United States of America on acid-free paper.

ISBN 9780991588640

Library of Congress Control Number 2015932510

A CIP catalogue record for this book is available from the British Library.

Murderesses
Two Italian Stories

Two Boyfriends Too Many

Sunday, July 8th, 2007

In the Passignano Woods, Rosa called over to her son for the thousandth time:

"Gianni! I thought I told you not to touch that ant's nest!"

"Leave him be!" muttered her husband, who was sat uncomfortably in a deck chair reading a newspaper. "He's doing no harm."

"He's spent the last half an hour poking around; soon or later he's going to get bitten," said Rosa.

"Well, let them bite; they're not poisonous!" replied the man. "And if he should get bitten, Gianni will never touch another ant's nest again. He's six years old; he's got to learn sooner or later."

"Help!" shouted a voice nearby.

"Did you hear that?" Rosa turned to her husband.

"I think I heard something, but I'm not really sure."

"Help!" shouted the voice again, and then they saw a blonde woman appear from behind the trees and start running towards them. At the same time they heard a shot. Whoever was shooting can't have been more than a hundred meters away.

"Oh my God!" cried Rosa. The blonde ran up to the tourists and collapsed, breathing heavily, onto a pile of dry leaves.

She was wearing a miniskirt and a sleeveless shirt open to the waist; so much of her beautiful body was on display, that had you asked anyone watching what her measurements were, not one person would have been wrong.

"Help me!" she said again, "there's a mad man over there! Didn't you hear the shot? He must have killed my boyfriend!"

"Good Gawd!" said Rosa. "I'm not going anywhere near him if he's armed!"

"I'll go," offered her husband.

"Don't be ridiculous!" screamed Rosa. "Do you want to get yourself killed?"

"Calm down. Wait here with Gianni and the young lady. Don't move."

He started walking slowly towards the woods leaving his wife screaming so hysterically that the young lady thought to calm her down by saying: "Don't worry, he won't shoot at your husband."

"What makes you so sure?"

"I think he's one of those mental cases that has it in for couples. I was alone with my boyfriend when he suddenly burst out of nowhere with a black scarf over his head, waving a pistol, and shouting that my boyfriend and I were sinners."

That would explain the open shirt. "How did you manage to escape?" asked Rosa, who disapproved of such exhibitionism in the young.

"I've got quick reactions, but my boyfriend wasn't able to move as quickly as me because...his belt was undone and his trousers fell down around his ankles."

"Disgusting!" thought Rosa, but she didn't say anything out loud because it was quite probable that one of the sinners was already dead. "Would you like something to drink?" she murmured instead.

"Some water would be lovely, thank you."

The blonde had just finished her water when Rosa's husband returned. "There's a young man dead over there.

I didn't see the killer; I didn't even hear him running away. I can't understand how he managed to disappear so quickly."

"Oh no!" shouted the blonde. "Oh God, no!"

She wasn't crying, but was obviously shocked. She fell back down to the ground and started pounding the dry leaves with her fists, screaming, "no, God, no."

Rosa and her husband looked at each other alarmed, while their child, unaware of the drama unfolding around him, stuck another stick into the nest.

"What shall we do?" she asked.

"The only logical thing we can do." replied her husband, "Call the police on my cell phone."

Monday, July 9th

At five o'clock in the afternoon, Police Inspector Aldo Parelli found himself at the five star Hotel Excelsior to talk to the young blonde who had had such a traumatic experience in the woods the day before.

"Madam," he said to the receptionist, "I came here yesterday to talk to Samantha Morelli, but the doctor told me that she was very shocked and wouldn't let me see her. However I really must see her today."

"That shouldn't be a problem," replied the receptionist, "the young lady has quite recovered from her shock. Yesterday she skipped dinner and at seven went out for a walk to take her mind off things. She came back very late. Today though she hasn't missed a meal."

"Could you tell her I'm here? Tell her that a police inspector is on his way up to ask her a few questions."

"Certainly. Room 319."

Samantha Morelli appeared tired, but even barefaced and pale she was the most beautiful creature that Parelli had ever seen. Blonde hair, sky-blue eyes, delicate features; she had the face of an angel, an angel with breasts and Miss Italia legs.

There wasn't any man alive who could have said, "she's not my type," other than those who only like dark-skinned brunettes.

"Forgive me," said the inspector, "but by law I have to take a written statement about what happened yesterday. I understand that you are still upset, but..."

"Please, take a seat," interrupted Samantha, to hurry things along.

Parelli obeyed. "How long had you known the victim?"

"For ten days. I met him on the first day of my holiday here."

"Really? Only ten days?"

"Yes, and it was a physical relationship. That's what you're getting at, isn't it?"

"Look, I'm here to establish the facts, not to pass judgement on anybody."

"Anyway, I would like you to know that I'm not that sort of girl; I would have married him. If he weren't dead."

The inspector smiled. "Was it love at first sight?"

"The worst kind."

"How did you meet him?"

"Didn't you know? Alfonso's the tour guide... I mean, he was the tour guide for the island excursions. The islands were the first things I wanted to see when I came here, and when I met Alfonso I went on the same excursion everyday. I imagine there are lots of other lovely things to see round here, but I've seen those islands nine times. Then one day we arranged to meet in those terrible woods."

Her voice shook, as if it was only then, in that moment, that she finally understood the horrendous events she was about to describe to the inspector. Yet the inspector was sure he heard a hint of sarcasm in voice when she said, “I imagine there are lots of other lovely things to see.”

“Now,” he said, “I know I’m asking a lot of you, but I need you to tell me exactly what happened in the woods. I’ve only got the statements from the witnesses who came to your aid.”

“I don’t see why you think my version will be any different from theirs. I was alone with Alfonso and we were messing around, but if you want to arrest me for committing an obscene act in public, I should warn you that no obscene act was committed. I’d only undone the top two buttons on my shirt when that madman appeared.”

She’s mocking me again, thought the inspector, which is strange as her pain is written all over her face.

“Could you tell me about the murderer?”

“There’s not much to tell. Medium build, a black scarf over his face. I wouldn’t recognise him if I saw him again. He was screaming about how we were sinners and that we had to die. I got away, but Alfonso couldn’t. He didn’t have his belt on and his trousers fell down.”

“How come nobody saw the killer running away?”

“I don’t know.”

“Do you know why he didn’t follow you? By your own account, Alfredo wasn’t the only one sinning.”

“Inspector, if you suspect that I shot him, please remember that I was already with the Fasone family when the shot was fired.”

“I know. They told me.”

“So I couldn’t have shot him, and please don’t ask me to get inside the head of a psychopath. Maybe he wanted to kill me, but couldn't. Or maybe he was shouting all this bullshit about sinners as a cover. Maybe he really only wanted to kill Alfonso."

"That's an interesting idea," said the inspector. "Hell, you should come and work for the police. I'll ask Alfonso's father if Alfonso had any enemies."

"Enemies?" Two tears rolled down her cheeks. "I think I am the one with enemies. Alfonso was a complete angel."

Parelli was confused. "Is there something you're not telling me?"

Samantha wiped away her tears. "Don't write this down. It's only an idea."

"Go on."

"My first boyfriend was killed too. I'm pretty well off financially; I've got lots of suitors, and I've turned down many a hand in marriage. A man I loved was killed yesterday. One plus one equals two, don't you see?"

The inspector was startled. "Your first boyfriend was killed? Where? In Rome?"

"Yes, in Rome. We were engaged."

"How long ago?"

"May twenty-fifth."

"Christ!"

"I know what you're thinking: that after a month I came here to find another man, but it wasn't like that. I came here to have a rest, Inspector, to forget that tragedy. But I met Alfonso and then this happened."

Her eyes glistened with tears again.

"Young lady, do you really believe that a disappointed suitor has decided to kill all of your boyfriends?"

"I don't know. There are a lot of crazy people out there. Anyway, there's no need to worry about my next boyfriend because there won't be another one."

"Don't be ridiculous, you're still very young!"

"I'm twenty-seven years old, and I feel like I've been widowed twice. No Inspector, fate has dictated that I forget about love and dedicate my life to other things. Well, going back to Alfonso... I would suggest that you ask around to see if anyone has seen a tourist that was only here in Passignano for a day. It might be the murderer."

"I will," said Parelli, "and I'll also be calling my colleagues in Rome, so don't be surprised if you get visit from a police officer once you're home. How long are you staying here?"

"At least until Alfonso's funeral. When will you release the body to the family?"

"We won't need much time. We already know that the bullet entered the chest, and from the entry wound we know that the killer was about as tall as the victim. The chest is an optimum target; if the bullet hits the heart, the victim dies immediately, but even if it hits a lung, within an hour the victim will be dead from internal bleeding. Alfonso was hit in the heart. There's not much more an autopsy will tell us."

Samantha nodded. "I'll stay here until Alfonso's funeral, then I'll go."

"As you wish," said the inspector, "and now you should rest. I'll leave you in peace. Thank you for talking to me about the murder. I'm sure the other couples in Passignano can sleep easy tonight."

In the doorway, he turned for a final time to admire Samantha's wan beauty, and said, "Can I ask you what you do in Rome?"

"I'm a writer."

It all now made perfect sense to Parelli. The way she spoke: elegant, studied, mocking; no, she wasn't an actress; she spoke as if she were writing a novel.

Wednesday, July 11th

Alfonso Mantegna's body lay in an open coffin, which was surrounded by relatives and friends. It didn't seem possible that such a handsome boy was dead: his skin, bronzed from a life spent under the sun, had yet to give way to white pallor of death.

Poor old thing, murmured his friends, he was only twenty five years old, if he hadn't been sneaking off into the woods with that slapper, none of this would have happened. No one knew Samantha, not even Alfonso's father, a widower, who was sat in the corner with a scowl on his face. The young victim had been seeing that little blonde from Rome for such a short time that he hadn't told anyone about her, or if he had, it would have been something along the lines of, "I've met this girl named Samantha, she's amazing," and nothing more.

Yet when Samantha Morelli made her entrance, everyone knew who she was. Who else could it have been? If it wasn't someone from Passignano, it had to be *that* girl.

Alfonso's father glared at her. "If it weren't for you, my son would still be alive," his eyes seemed to say, but Samantha, not in the least intimidated, didn't hesitate. She stopped in front of him, a small ivory-coloured satin cushion in her hands.

"Signor Mantegna?"

"Yes?"

"My name's Samantha. I was wondering whether you would allow me to give this small token to your son. I loved him so much."

"It's all your fault, you whore," said a voice in the old man's head, but his lips didn't move.

"Please?" the young woman's voice shook. "I doubt you'll believe me, but Alfonso and I, we were going to get married. I would like him to have something of mine to take with him. It's only trifle, look."

She showed the cushion to the old man; it was beautiful, Alfonso's initials were on it, embroidered in gold. Good Lord, he thought, how had she got hold of something like that so quickly? And why didn't the funeral home suggest it to me, his father?

The cushion was too beautiful to be thrown away, so the old man grudgingly gave his consent.

The girl went up to the open coffin, gently lifted up the head of the dead man, and put the cushion underneath. Then she kissed Alfonso's forehead, and although much had been whispered about that 'whore from Rome,' not one of those present dared separate her from her lover.

Friday, July 13th

At the villa in Olgiata, Inspector Tommaso Marini looked around, fascinated. The housekeeper had told him to wait in the sitting room, where the paintings, tapestries, silver trays with gold edgings, and beautifully restored antique furniture would have made even the most experienced art thief weak at the knees with desire.

When the owner of the objects arrived, the inspector felt his heartbeat quicken. They had told him that Samantha was beautiful, and he had expected to see a woman devoid of physical defects. The creature in front of him though, not only was she perfect, she had that luminosity that only the intellectually brilliant possess.

He got up from the sofa and shook her hand. “Nice to meet you. Tommaso Marini,” he said, forgetting for a moment that he was a police inspector.

Samantha smiled at his confusion. “Yes, Inspector,” she said, “I know who you are, and I know that you’ve come because you’ve got news from Passignano. Please, take a seat.”

Marini sat back down on the sofa. He was used to intimidating the people he had to interrogate, but here he had the distinct impression that the boot was on the other foot. He tried his utmost to not think about the beauty of the woman sat opposite him, and began:

“Well, madam. Your statement to the police has forced us to reopen the case of the murder of the lawyer Onorio Cristaldi, which took place at his villa a month and a half ago. This man was also in a relationship with you?”

“We were engaged,” clarified Samantha.

“Quite. But at the time we all agreed: the motive was burglary. But you, madam, didn’t put forward any other theories.”

“Of course not — why should I? My second fiancé was still alive. But this second murder makes me see things differently. Things that I hadn’t seen before.”

“Very well. You’re now going to hear a statement taken from the lawyer’s housekeeper after she had found his body.” The inspector pulled a piece of paper out of his pocket, and started to read: ‘The young lady, Samantha Morelli, had left half an hour before. I’m sure because I saw her drive off in her car. As it was dinnertime, I went into the kitchen to prepare something for the lawyer; then I heard a shot that came from upstairs. I’m old and I can’t get up the stairs like I used to, but I did my best to get to the office as soon as I could. The lawyer was on the floor, dead, and the safe was open and completely empty. The window was open too; that's how the thief must have got in. I looked out of the window and I saw a man running away. He was wearing overalls and had a hat on his head. I imagine it was easy for him to climb up to the first floor.' End of the statement," said the inspector. "I might add that the lawyer kept a pistol in his office to defend himself from thieves, but the weapon has disappeared and hasn't been found. He could well have been murdered by his own gun. There was money in the safe, and a number of documents concerning his clients. The thief took everything."

"Inspector," said Samantha, "why are you boring me by telling me things I already know?"

"Okay, *you* tell *me*. What has changed? Why shouldn't Cristaldi's murder not be motivated by burglary? A jealous rival wouldn't know the combination to the safe, neither would he be able to open and empty it so quickly. We're talking about a professional thief here."

"Yes, I know, but now another man who was in a relationship with me has died," insisted Samantha. "Do you believe in coincidences?"

"Very well. You're convinced it's a suitor. Would you mind telling me who it is so I can get back to work?"

"Oh, no!" said Samantha, "I can't go around accusing people. I've rejected at least ten suitors over the last six months, and if one of those is a crazy killer, it's up to the police to find out which one."

"Ten in six months? Aren't you exaggerating a little?"

"Do you think I'm megalomaniac? You will have the name and addresses of all these people," said Samantha, annoyed. "And now *I* have a question for *you*: do you know who my father was?"

“Of course I do. Eugenio Morelli, the plastic surgeon.”

“Do you know how much a plastic surgeon earns?”

“I have a vague idea.”

“My father died over two months ago. I am the only heir, the only one. Do know what that means in this country? I started to receive all these marriage proposals when Papa was diagnosed with a tumor. Even if I had been a dwarf in a circus they would have asked me to marry them.”

The inspector smiled. “I see. For your money? Even if she were penniless, a beauty like yourself would be overwhelmed by suitors.” The compliment had slipped out before he could stop it, but Samantha accepted it without batting an eyelid.

“That’s why you should believe me. Don’t you think that a man would kill because he has lost all of this, or do you think he would be motivated by the hope of having it?” She waved her hand around the room, pointing at the furniture and paintings, but also at her body, and suddenly Marini decided that she wasn’t a megalomaniac after all.

“I’ll look into it,” he promised.

Thursday, June 28th 2007

Alfonso was a good looking man, used to receiving flirty looks from the tourists who climbed aboard his boat, but as soon as he saw Samantha, he knew that something important was about to happen to him. There she was, stood squarely on the deck of the boat, enchanting him, staring at him and smiling so openly that he felt compelled to ignore social conventions and speak to her.

"Are you for real, or are you something I've dreamt up after a heavy night out?" He would never, ever have gone up to a client especially one who was so obviously much further up on the social ladder.

But she smiled and replied: "I am real. Are you?"

From that moment on, they were inseparable. The girl went on the same trip every day; the islands no longer had any secrets from her. There were many other tourists on the boat however, and it wasn't easy for the two youngsters to talk privately; when Alfonso was doing his job as a tour guide, he had to address the whole group.

On the way back from the ninth excursion, she stayed on deck, waiting until she felt the presence of a body behind her, and heard a voice whisper in her ear:

"I've got to have you. I know that's what you want too. For pity's sake, tell me when and where. I'm free on Sundays, all day.

Samantha smiled, and with one of her dainty fingers pointed to a building on the shore. "See that hotel? That's where I'm staying."

"Okay."

"There's a small woods very close to the hotel."

"Yes."

"We could meet at the hotel. Room number 319. And then we can go into the woods. I don't think it's a good idea to do certain things in my room. Everyone would know."

"I wouldn't do it in your room either," replied the boy, "I know all the staff."

"Do you?"

"My parents used to run it. Then my Mum died and my father retired. The management changed a couple of years ago."

"Now I sleep there. What a coincidence," murmured Samantha. She should have said: *I know, I know everything; my parents came here on holiday, to this very hotel as newlyweds, and they came back when I was small. My parents knew your parents.*

But that remained her secret. All she said was: "That's organised then. I'll be waiting for you. Sunday the eighth at half past four."

Thursday, July 19th

Inspector Marini was shown into Samantha's sitting room for the second time and watched her come in. "I hope I'm not disturbing you," he said, politely.

"I was writing," she replied.

"If you'd rather, I could return in an hour or so."

"It wouldn't make any difference. When I write, I work for twelve hours a day. A visit at anytime during the day is a disturbance."

"Thank you for being so honest." The inspector smiled. "I came to tell you that you were right. I asked for the bullet that killed Alfonso Mantegna, and I compared it to the one they took out of Cristaldi's chest. Would you believe they are the same: they were shot with the same weapon!"

Samantha tilted her head to one side as if to say 'I told you so.'

"Where is the gun?" she asked.

"Only the murderer knows. Anyway, it's clear enough that we have two murders in two different cities, committed by the same person."

The girl nodded.

"Now," continued the inspector, "let's start with the

list you gave me. Here are the names of eleven men who have all proposed, or made sexual overtures, or anything else of a similar nature. You gave me these eleven names and also specified the date on which the said advances took place. Nine of the eleven men proposed when your father was dying, while two are suitors from before then. Is that correct?"

"Yes."

"We've checked their alibis. Not for the first crime, as no one remembers where they were on May twenty-fifth, but seeing that the same person carried out both the crimes, we asked where people were on Sunday, July eighth. Ten people have watertight alibis. Sundays are usually spent in the company of family and friends. Only one person on the list didn't have an alibi, madam."

Samantha raised an eyebrow. "Only one? Who?"

"Stefano Baschi."

She was shocked. "Stefano?" It can't be him. He wouldn't hurt a fly. We went to school together, first middle school and then high school. He adores me. He's always wanted me, but me, not my money."

"Madam, you included him on the list, and unfortunately he's the only one who hasn't got an alibi. He says that on Sunday, July 8, he was at home, alone. His neighbors were out and about, so nobody can confirm whether he was at home or not."

"Oh, the misfortune of living alone!" cried Samantha, "Stefano is an orphan, he was brought up by his aunts. On his eighteenth birthday, he decided to go to live alone in the house he inherited from his parents. The only person who could provide him with an alibi is his cat."

"That's all very well. He may be unlucky, but we'll still have to search his home. His lack of alibi doesn't necessarily mean he's guilty, but if we were to find a clue in his house, then obviously it would change things," said the inspector.

"What do you hope to find?" asked Samantha, "The murder weapon? Stefano would never be so stupid as to keep it in it house. That's if, that's *if* he does have it."

"Madam, you never know what you might find. You could find the times of the coaches from Perugia to Passignano written in a diary. Or even a shrine with candles lit in front of a photo of Samantha Morelli. I'll ask the judge for a search warrant."

Samantha shrugged but said nothing more.

"I see. Stefano is a good friend of yours and you don't think he's guilty, but you were the one who opened this can of worms. Now you'll have to face the consequences."

Wednesday, July 25th

Inspector Marini's girlfriend, Brigida, was a psychologist who was frequently called upon by the police for her expertise. As a consultant. For the last couple of years she had got used to being ignored by her boyfriend when he was busy at work, only hearing from him, sometimes four or five times a day, when he was in need of her professional opinion.

So when he invited her out to dinner on a Wednesday evening, which was neither an anniversary nor a holiday, Brigida was certain that her boyfriend had a worrying case on his hands, and wanted some advice.

The restaurant terrace was charming, the menu was optimum, but for once Brigida found Tommaso's case more interesting than her surroundings.

"So," the inspector continued, between one prawn

and the next, "we've searched Baschi's house, and we found, hidden among his winter socks, a Rolex watch with the initials OC written on the back. Now, even supposing he could afford a Rolex — he works in the post office but has practically nothing in the bank — his initials aren't OC. The percentage of persons whose name starts with O is pretty low, which is why I immediately showed the watch to Onorio Cristaldi's housekeeper and asked her whether she had seen it before. When she saw it she cried, "It's the lawyer's watch, his girlfriend gave it to him. It disappeared the evening he was robbed."

"Perfect," said Brigida.

"Almost too perfect, and that's why I need your help. The reactions of the main players when I confronted them with this piece of evidence don't convince me. Point one: the reaction of Samantha Morelli, when I gave her the news. First of all she said: "It can't be Stefano, he's not that stupid." When I pointed out to her that this watch didn't just magically appear in his sock drawer, and as he lives on the seventh floor, it's extremely unlikely that an enemy of hers could have climbed all the way up and entered through the window, she said: "poor Stefano," had a bit of a cry and asked whether her friend would have to be arrested. "Of course," I replied, "as soon as I get a warrant." And then she...you'll never guess what she said next — she complained that his cat would be left to fend for itself if Stefano was sent to prison. She said: "if no one wants to look after that cat, get them to bring it here."

"A sensitive soul," commented Brigida.

"It's all very well being sensitive now, but she was the one who led me to the murderer. Why is she sorry now?"

"I'd imagine," said the psychologist, "that she thought

it was another of her suitors. One that she'd found overbearing. Yes, that's it. She wanted to send someone to prison, but not Baschi. She never once imagined that it was him, and so the news has upset her."

Marini thought for a long moment. "Yes, it's plausible," he said. "Now explain Baschi's reaction. He didn't bat an eyelid when he saw the search warrant, he seemed so sure that we wouldn't find anything. But the colour drained from his face in front of my very eyes when he saw the watch. Obviously he said that he had never seen the watch before, that someone must have put it in his winter sock drawer, knowing full well that he would never open it in summer. Anyone in his position would have said the same thing, but I think I believe him. Someone with a first class degree wouldn't be so stupid as to keep his victim's watch. Initialled, to boot."

"He lives on the seventh floor, you said so yourself," said Brigida, perplexed, "who could have put it there?"

"I have no idea. And that's not all. I went to see him in prison yesterday."

Tuesday, July 24th

In the prison visitor's room, the inspector saw Stefano Baschi again. He was a young man, slim, and blessed with two magnificent brown eyes, which were almost the same colour as his hair. That Samantha had turned down such a handsome suitor struck him as odd, even if she did seem fond of him, but that wasn't why Marini was there.

"Signor Baschi," he said, "I've been told that you haven't appointed a defense lawyer."

Stefano gave a slight nod.

"I'm here today to tell you that the court has appointed a lawyer on your behalf. His name is Giovanni Calazi, and he will be here tomorrow during visiting hours."

"I won't agree to see him," said Stefano.

"What do you mean you won't see him?"

"I have no intention of speaking to any defense lawyer. Once the trial date has been set, then I'll see him three or four days before the trial, but not before."

"Are you mad? What kind of defense can he prepare in three days?"

"There's no defense to prepare because I haven't done anything. And anyway, if Samantha wants me to go to prison, I'll go to prison."

Marini stopped, shocked.

"Whatever gave you the idea that Samantha wants you in prison? Have I ever said that she has accused you of anything? Actually, if you really want to know, Samantha doesn't think that you're guilty."

"Really? Then what's she playing at?"

"What do you mean Signor Baschi?"

But Stefano didn't say anything else. He put his head in his hands and sobbed.

Marini felt uncomfortable. "Signor Baschi," he tried again, "could you please explain to me why you said that Samantha wanted you in prison?"

"Take no notice of what I said."

"But it's important!"

Stefano dried his tears and shook his head. "You won't get another word out of me. Neither you, nor that lawyer you want me to talk to."

"But Signor Baschi, your behavior is —"

"Do you think I'm insane? Prove it. Now, if you don't mind, I'd like to return to my cell."

Marini signaled to the guards that he had finished, and the prisoner was taken away. The inspector felt somewhat startled by what he had heard.

He didn't understand. He had had the sensation that Stefano had burst into tears because Samantha didn't think he was guilty.

Obviously it was the reaction of a man in love. But was it the reaction of an innocent man? That he would have to find out.

"Yes, it is odd," said Brigida, "and not only what he said is strange. If someone believes they are innocent, why do they refuse to see a lawyer?"

"Because he is convinced that he has to take the blame to save his beloved?" ventured the inspector.

"But didn't you tell me that she had a watertight alibi?"

"Yes, she has. And I've got no evidence against Stefano other than that stupid watch. No one saw him at Passignano. His photo was displayed at all the train and coach stations: no one recognized him."

"If he was there to kill someone, he could have gone in disguise."

"That's true, but if were the judge, I couldn't convict him on the basis of a watch found in the drawer and no alibi. If a man commits a crime of passion, and then tries to cover his tracks by pretending it was a robbery, he doesn't keep the stolen goods: he gets rid of them."

"Passion?" cried Brigida, "did you say a crime of passion? Oh my God, that's it! Baschi…could have committed the crime in Rome but not the crime in Passignano!"

"I'm not following you," said Marini.

"Listen. To commit the second crime, Baschi would have had to have known that Samantha was flirting with a tour guide. Tommaso, how could Stefano have known about a relationship that only lasted ten days? Was he following her? Spying on her? If he had been there, people would have seen him. Do you think he slept in his car?"

"No," replied the inspector, "Baschi was seen in Rome until July seventh. The only day he doesn't have an alibi is Sunday the eighth. Why didn't I think of that? Who could have told him that Samantha..."

"Something smells fishy," says Brigida, "and I'm not talking about the prawns."

Friday, July 27th

"The young lady is upstairs," said Samantha's housekeeper, "I think she's writing. Would you like to wait in the sitting room?"

"Not today," said the inspector, "I'm not here to speak to the young lady. I want to speak to you."

"Me? Why, Inspector?"

"Because you might be able to tell me something that the young lady hasn't told me, and quite probably, never will tell me. There must be another man involved in this business. Can I have a word with you somewhere Samantha won't hear us?"

The housekeeper closed the hall door. "She won't be able to hear us here," she said, "but I can't see how I can help you."

"Listen. Samantha has lost two fiancés in forty days. First of all, could you tell me if she has ever had others?"

"No, never."

Her reply perplexed Marini. “Are you sure? A beautiful twenty-seven year-old girl like Samantha? Not even casual boyfriends?”

“Never. And I’m sure because I’ve been working in this villa since Samantha was born.”

“Christ!” murmured the inspector, “she’s turned down over ten men, and some, in my opinion, were pretty good catches. Tell me what you know about this affair.”

“Samantha only thinks about writing. She wants to become a famous writer; she’s not interested in anything else.”

“Is that what the young lady told you?”

“She tells pretty much everybody the same thing.”

“So why did she start a relationship with the lawyer as soon as her father died? Was she lonely? Do you think she was depressed? Was Cristaldi very attractive?”

“Oh, for heaven’s sake,” replied the housekeeper, “ he was a fifty year-old bachelor, he was losing his hair and gaining a big waist.”

At this point, the inspector was so confused that he felt nauseous; he felt as if he was staring at a cockroach swimming in a bowl of minestrone soup.

“Let me get this straight. Samantha tells everyone that she’s not interested in men, but then the minute her father dies, she gets engaged to an ugly little man who’s twice her age. Am I right?”

“I think she was secretly seeing him a month before her father died. I overheard her on the phone. I wasn’t eavesdropping or anything, but Samantha wanders around the house with her phone glued to her ear. When the doctor died, they got engaged.”

“I imagine that the girl thought her father wouldn’t

have approved of such an old son in law, and that's why she didn't tell him."

"I've got no idea. It's not as if they had only just met! Cristaldi was Doctor Morelli's lawyer."

A bowl of minestrone soup full of cockroaches appeared before the inspector's eyes. They were laughing and waving at him as they swam around the bowl.

"I haven't got a clue what's going on," muttered the inspector, "she says no to the boys and chooses her father's lawyer. Fifty years old. It wasn't about money because she was richer than he was. And then as soon as he dies, she hooks up with a penniless kid! Did you know that her second boyfriend was two years younger than Samantha?"

"The one from Passignano?"

"Yes. By the way, the young lady said that she went on holiday to forget about the death of Cristaldi. What the hell made her choose the lake at Tresimano? Did someone recommend it to her?"

"No, Samantha knows Passignano. Her parents took her on holiday there when she was a little girl."

"Ah. So it's possible that Samantha had met the young man who was killed before?"

"Let me think... No, no. Samantha was around two the last time the Morelli family went on holiday there."

"Two years old. Alfonso would have just been born, damn it!" shouted the inspector. "She goes there at the end of June and immediately falls in love with that boy! Do you think she's the type who falls in love that easily?"

"I've already told you she isn't," replied the woman, "Samantha is only interested in her books. I doubt she would have married the lawyer or the boy from Passignano. I know her very well, she isn't the type to want a family. That's why I thought those engagements were very odd."

"I think they were odd too. But what if Samantha's changed? What if she had a nervous breakdown and has gone a little crazy," ventured the inspector. The housekeeper shook her head. "There have been no problems with her nerves, Inspector. I've never seen her angry, I've never seen her cry over trifles. She's incredibly sensible. A computer with legs."

"Speaking of computers, what type of books does she write?"

"Fiction, but I've never read any of it."

"Is there anything you could tell me about the young lady's work?"

"One thing I do know is that she needed the inheritance money from her father to open a publishing house. Now that she's paid the inheritance tax, I don't think it'll be long before she does."

"Are you sure? Nobody opens a publishing house just to publish their own work."

"She doesn't want to publish her own books," replied the housekeeper. "Samantha graduated in languages, she's an expert in French literature, and she wants to publish some French authors in Italy. Don't ask me which ones, I don't understand anything about literature. There's a bookcase full of French novels in the library. I dust them off every Saturday."

The inspector nodded thoughtfully. "You've been most helpful madam," he said. "Thank you."

That evening he called Brigida and told her everything.

"So," he concluded, "an intelligent young lady decides to dedicate her life to literature. She turns down a handful of marriage proposals, including a number with good prospects, and I should know because I met every single one, and the architect Novelli and the professor Gallo weren't bad, neither physically nor intellectually. Anyway, Samantha turned them all down because she doesn't want anything to get in the way of her beloved books. But while her father is dying, she starts a relationship with a fifty year-old baldie. The man dies, she plays the part of a desperate widow who books a holiday to try to get over the tragedy, but the body of her first fiancé is still warm in his coffin when she sneaks off into the woods to fuck the local tour guide, a boy who will never be her social or intellectual equal. Brigida, you're the psychologist. Do you think Samantha has psychological issues?"

"No," replied the expert, "and if you want the truth, I don't think the tourist guide was the only person she was fucking around with. I think she's taking you all for a ride."

May 1994

Samantha and Stefano Baschi sat next to one another in class in the fourth year of high school. Neither one was paying much attention to the algebra lesson they were supposed to be following. Stefano, in a state of rapture, was staring at the girl seated next to him, while Samantha was reading a book under the desk that had nothing whatsoever to do with algebra.

"What are you reading?" whispered the boy.

"A French novel."

"What's it called?"

"*La Poupèe Sanglante* by Gaston Leroux."

"Isn't there a translation?"

"No, that's why I'm reading it in French."

"Do you understand it?"

"What do you think? You know I'm good at French."

"Why are you reading it now?"

"Because Maths is such a drag and I want to know how the story ends. I'm on the last chapter."

"What's it about?"

"You two!" shouted the algebra teacher, "either you stop talking, or I'll send you both to the headmaster's office. Is that clear?"

The students were silent. A quarter of an hour later, the bell rang for recreation and Stefano asked Samantha to tell him more about the book.

"It's fantastic!" she said. "It's about a poet with a sensitive soul who falls in love with a girl called Christine, but he's ugly, very ugly, and she can't bear to even look at him. Then one day he's condemned to death and killed for a murder he didn't commit. Christine's father, a scientist, steals the dead man's brain and sticks it into the head of a robot he's created. The robot has a body that resembles a humans, a beautiful face, and now he has the brain of a poet. Christine falls in love with him.

"Sounds like a shitty science fiction novel," commented Stefano.

"That's what you always say, but wait until you hear how it finishes. There's an existential crisis no less in this trashy novel. The poet's dreams have come true: Christine loves him. But then he realizes that he hasn't got a body to love her with, as his body isn't made from flesh and blood. The scientist had programmed his robot to think autonomously, but he never thought that his brain would go beyond certain limits; that it would be capable of reflecting on his limitations and decide to auto-destruct! So when the robot hears Christine declare her love for him," Samantha's voice breaks with emotion, "a love that could never be reciprocated, he realizes that he has to set her free and throws himself off a rock to his death. Christine looks over the cliff edge and but doesn't see a body, only pieces of metal and screws. That was her beloved. Could you imagine anything worse?" She breathed. "You can't love someone with only your soul, and neither can you love someone with only your body: you need both of those things together. The book, however much it may seem to be a science fiction novel, has a lot to teach us. And there's not a single publisher in Italy who has bothered to publish this masterpiece!"

Her excitement had transformed the young woman's face, bringing a colour to her cheeks that made her, if it were possible, even more beautiful than usual. Stefano, enraptured, stared at her without replying.

"Were you listening to what I said?" she asked, annoyed, despite the fact that the eyes that fixed her belonged to such a handsome young man.

"No, I wasn't actually."

"Why not?"

"Because I love you." And that was the first time he told her.

Monday, July 30th, 2007

Onorio Cristaldi died leaving just one heir, his sister, who inherited his villa. The lady, however, didn't have the slightest intention of living in such an expensive place — the maintenance costs and taxes were sky high — so the property had been put on the market and the housekeeper had found work with another family.

Inspector Marini, who already knew her new address as he had tracked her down to show her the infamous watch, went back to ask her a few more questions.

"Do you know whether Signor Cristaldi had any other girlfriends before starting a relationship with Samantha Morelli?"

"Not to my knowledge, Inspector," said the old lady, "I was with the lawyer for ten years, and I can tell you he never brought a lady home with him, not even for lunch. To be honest, and you must forgive me for saying this, but I thought he was gay. Then along came Samantha and I knew I had been mistaken."

"Why did he choose Samantha? Do you think he was a man motivated by money? Was it that important that he waited fifty years to find a woman who was rich enough?"

The housekeeper shrugged. "Maybe. Or maybe he had never known the joy of sex before Samantha came along and opened his eyes."

She's no housekeeper, thought Marini, she's a psychologist, and she could give Brigida a few pointers while she's at it.

"Do you think she was in love with him?"

"In love? I don't know. I always got the impression that she was as cold as ice. And anyway, no one would have called the gentleman good looking, poor thing, or even particularly interesting."

"Hence you don't understand Samantha's interest in Signor Cristaldi," said Marini.

"No, I never understood why. She came here, took him into the bedroom, and when they had finished, she left immediately. She wouldn't even stop for a cup of tea. It was like having a hooker in the house, if you pardon the term."

That detail was a stain on the beautiful picture of Samantha's character that the Inspector had lovingly painted in his head.

"I would now like to ask you a difficult question," he said, "but you might already know the answer. Doctor Morelli was a plastic surgeon. Why did he need a lawyer? Did he have any financial interests to protect? Did he need advice about investments?"

"I don't know," said the woman, "but I know how they met. Signor Cristaldi told everyone because it was such a funny story."

"Go on."

"It was all down to one of Doctor Morelli's patients. He had reshaped her nose, but she wasn't happy with the result," the housekeeper smiled, "she wanted it smaller so took the Doctor to court. Now her face was as long as a horse's and the Doctor proved that a tiny nose on that long face would have been ridiculous. You can only imagine how the judge must have laughed when they showed him all the different types of noses..."

"I see," said the inspector, "the lawyer won the case and they became friends."

"Yes, but they didn't see each other very often. The last time the Doctor came here, they had already found the tumor in his lung. He was very thin, unrecognizable even. I never saw again."

"So he was ill and went to visit his lawyer," said the inspector almost to himself. He was thoughtful for a moment, then changed the subject. "Going back to the evening of the robbery —"

"Oh no!" cried the woman, "I've told you that story a hundred times! What else do you need to know?"

"One more thing. You saw the thief running away,

but normally when a thief enters a building that they know is occupied, they bring reinforcements. Did you notice if the thief, after he had jumped over the gates, climbed into a car? If there was an accomplice who was waiting for him in the car?"

"No, Inspector. He escaped on foot. I watched him running off from the window."

"Wasn't he struggling to carry all the stuff he had stolen?"

"His bag wouldn't have been heavy."

"What makes you think that?"

"I know how big the safe was." replied the woman, "It didn't have any silver in it, and as there were no women living in the house, there were no jewels either. I think the lawyer only kept banknotes and certain documents in there and it would have all fitted inside a supermarket carrier bag."

"Was the safe completely empty?"

"Yes Inspector, small, wide open, and empty."

"Strange," said the inspector.

"Why is it strange?"

"The thief was seen by the lawyer and shot him, meaning that he would have been in a hurry to leave. Why then did he waste valuable time stealing documents with no value whatsoever? And another thing: was Cristaldi's watch in the safe?"

"That I don't know. When you showed it to me last week, it was the first time I'd seen it in ages."

"The watch was in this young man's house," said Marini, taking a photo of Stefano Baschi out of his pocket, "take a good look at him. Does his build match that of the person you saw running away?"

The old lady stared at the photo of Stefano on the

beach in his swimming trunks.

"Maybe. I don't know, I think the thief was thinner, but he was wearing such baggy clothes it was difficult to tell. Is that one of the young men Samantha turned down?"

"Yes."

"Well, the girl's a idiot then. Imagine choosing Cristaldi over such a handsome young man."

The inspector sighed and put the photo back into his pocket.

"Thank you madam. You've been a great help."

June 2001

On the beach in Ostia, Samantha was reading a newspaper under an umbrella. Stefano sat down next to her and said: "Well, have you decided yet?"

"I've decided that I'm not going."

"Come on Samantha! I'm only asking you to come dancing with me. Some of our old classmates will be there; the disco belongs to Roberta Pratelli's father."

"That's exactly why I'm not going! I don't want to see our old classmates! They'll ask me what I've been up to. What am I supposed to say to them? That I haven't achieved anything, that's what!"

"Sweetheart, you're twenty-one years old, you're about to get a major in languages, and you call that nothing? You've still got loads of time to change the world."

"Fine. I'm twenty-one years old and I've written a really good novel that's been turned down by three editors. Where I come from, we call that failure."

"There will be at least another ten."

"Please Stefano, leave me alone. I'm in no mood for your advice. See this magazine? I've just read the book review page; some bastard has written a really gushing review for a book that is a complete load of rubbish. I don't know how these things work: is he bribed to write certain reviews? Or, as they have only got space for four reviews a month, does he only read the four books written by relatives of the editor, and therefore is forced to write good reviews? They don't review any other books, because they don't read any other books, that's for sure."

No, it really wasn't a good time to invite her to the disco, but maybe it was the right time to get her to open up a little, so with this in mind, Stefano lay down on the sand next to her.

"What are you going to do about it then? Have you got a plan?"

"I might have."

"Do you want to talk about it?"

"Only if you don't call me a crazy fool."

"I'll do my best."

"Okay. This is what I'm going to do. I'm the only daughter of a rich father, and when he dies, I'll be able to live comfortably off my inheritance. I'll have a beautifully furnished house and I don't intend to buy anything else, so I'll never manage to spend all of it. I have no intention of giving any of it to charity, no, I'll open a publishing house and I'll call it Editrice Autonoma, and the books will be initialed EA. I'll start by publishing all those fantastic French novels that have never been published in Italy."

"Like *La Poupèe Sanglante*?"

"Oh. You remember *La Poupèe Sanglante*? Well, Gaston Leroux might have been my idol when I was younger, but I've discovered that there are much better authors out there. *Becket* by Jean Anouilh, *Le Sagouin* by Mauriac, the Marcel Pagnol comedies, Jean Cocteau tragedies, and there are five or six fantastic novels by Françoise Sagan that are practically unknown in Italy. Either Italian editors don't know what fantastic literature is, or they haven't got the courage to take a punt on an unknown author."

"Did you read all of these authors in French?"

"Yes. I'm writing my thesis on Jean Cocteau, because not only did he write books, he dabbled in cinema too. There's a lot to write about him. Anyway, if I ever manage to open a successful publishing house that publishes the classics. I'll start to bring out books by an unknown French author called something like Marie Larmont."

"So you'll be writing under a pseudonym," said Stefano.

"Exactly. I'll publish my books and pay a journalist to write fabulous things about this Marie Larmont, literary genius."

"Will you ever reveal yourself as the real author?"

"Only when Marie Larmont is famous and I'm old. How satisfying it will be to play them at their own game, and win. Those Italian critics who gush over books that aren't worth the paper they're printed on won't know what's hit them."

Stefano sighed. "Samantha," he said, "Are you sure you won't lose money? I mean, not because your books won't be any good, but because people don't read much, and I doubt they'll give two hoots about Pagnol and Cocteau."

"I've thought about that," she replied, "and it's a risk I'm ready to take. I've got the money, and I'm not interested in anything else. Obviously, I'm not going to sit around at home doing nothing, I don't want children, and you won't see me teaching French in a school. I only love books, Stefano. Do you understand?"

The two youngsters looked at one another. Stefano's soul sank into her blue eyes. "Yes," was his reply. He could read that funny little brain of hers, and he understood what she wanted, even though the truth hurt. He saw her future, and he wasn't part of it.

Friday, August 3rd, 2007

Inspector Marini thought it would be a good idea to spend a weekend in Passignano at the same hotel Samantha had stayed at.

By speaking to the people who had met her, he should be able to gain useful information on the case, information that had a habit of coming out when you least expected it to. For example, one of the maids referred to the fact that when she arrived, Samantha had the air of someone who was looking to enjoy herself, and didn't look like a woman heartbroken by the death of a fiancé.

Not wishing to leave any stone unturned, Marini also went to talk to Alfonso Mantegna's father and asked him if he had ever met the by now famous blonde who had been in a relationship with his son.

"I only saw her once," replied the old man, "she had the cheek to come to the funeral."

"Did Alfonso talk to you about her?"

"No. My son and I never talked about those kind of things."

"Why?"

"Does it matter? Alfredo's dead."

"Signor Mantegna, anything could be important for this investigation."

"Alfonso was very close to his mother, she was the

one he talked to. She died when he was fifteen years old, a difficult age, and I... Well, I didn't try to take her place in my son's heart. I left his friends and schoolmates to fill the gap she left."

"Why?"

"Do I have to tell you? Fine. He wasn't really *my* son."

A strange chill ran up the inspector's spine as he waited for the old man to continue his story.

"My wife and I had tried many times to have a child, and although tests revealed that her hormone levels were normal and everything was working as it should be, I refused to be tested because... I was ashamed. It's awful when you know that your wife wants a child and you have to tell her that you're infertile. But then curiosity got the better of me, and I had the tests done, and I was the one who was infertile, but I never told my wife. Then one day, when she was forty years old, she told me she was pregnant. What could I have done? I couldn't do anything. I pretended to be happy, to believe that the baby was mine. I don't regret what I did because when she died, I was, to all intents and purposes, a widower with a handsome, intelligent son. And at least Patrizia had the joy of being a mother before she died, and I hadn't been the one to deny her that sacred right. For what it's worth, she loved me, and only cheated on me that one time to get pregnant. We were happy together. Anyway, why am I supposed to be telling you all this?"

"I won't tell a single living soul," said the inspector. "Now I understand why you weren't Alfonso's confidante, but what did you know about him? For example, was he the type whose head was turned by money? The girl he was with was very rich."

"Was Samantha Prizzi rich? I didn't even know that."

"Her name isn't Prizzi," said the inspector, "what made you think it was?"

"That's the name she gave to my son. It's the only thing I do know. The day it all happened, Alfonso told me that he was going to spend the afternoon with a charming girl from Rome called Samantha Prizzi. Or was it Pozzi?"

"No sir, you're mistaken. Her actual name is Samantha Morelli."

The old man started. "No, that's not the name Alfonso gave me; I would have remembered that name. Morelli was a famous plastic surgeon who used to come here on holiday years ago. He was one of my customers."

"That's right. Samantha is his daughter. She wanted to return to the same place where her parents vacationed. Signor Mantegna! What's the matter? Are you alright?"

The old man was shaking from head to foot; if he had been standing, he would have fallen over. After a couple of minutes he said, "Samantha Morelli! I'd much rather he were dead than marry her. Yes, I'd rather he were dead."

"I don't understand," murmured Marini, "would you mind telling me why?"

Monday, August 6th

The Inspector sat down in Samantha's sitting room. There was not a hint of a smile on his face, not even when he saw the lady of the house enter. One glance was enough to tell her that something was up.

"I know all about you, young lady," said Marini.

"Are you sure?" Seemingly unconcerned, she sat down on the sofa and crossed her shapely legs. "Tell me what you know about me. Under what pseudonym will I publish my books?"

"This is no laughing matter. I know the motive for both the murders: I've spoken to Alfonso Mantegna's father."

"So?"

"So Alfonso would have been Alfonso Morelli, if he had been recognized by his real father. The boy was your brother, and you knew, which is why you gave him a false name. You told him your surname was Prizzi, because you thought that someone could have told him who his father was, and that he wouldn't have gone into the woods to have sex with his sister."

"Excuse me, are you saying that I went to Passignano to have sex with my brother? Do you think I'm that depraved?"

"No, you never intended to consummate the relationship. You took Alfonso into the woods to kill him.

"You're forgetting that there are two witnesses who saw me half-undressed and shocked when Alfonso was still alive. I was with them when the shot was fired."

"I've thought about that. I believe you killed Alfonso with a pistol with a silencer, then you lit a firecracker, then you ran out of the woods. When the witnesses heard the bang from the firecracker, Alfonso was already dead. This would explain the mysterious disappearance of the killer; there was no one else in the woods except you and Alfonso."

Samantha laughed. "Inspector, if you had proof of any of this, we wouldn't be here right now. I would be at the station being given the third degree. But if you think that's what happened, feel free to investigate. Go and look for evidence of a firecracker in the woods. Firecrackers leave their mark."

"I will. This story makes more sense than the one about the crazy suitor. Stefano Baschi couldn't have known that you were at Passignano and that you had found yourself a lover. No, Stefano could never have known, which is why he didn't have a reason to kill Alfonso."

"And what was my motive, Inspector?"

"Your father's will. His money. I'm pretty sure you would have lost quite a bit of money to his illegitimate son."

"My father didn't leave a will. I'm the only heir, I've already paid inheritance tax on the money."

"Don't try to be clever with me young lady. You destroyed his will. It was in Onorio Cristaldi's safe. Your father didn't have any legal problems; he had no need for a lawyer. Why then, did he rush to Cristaldi's house the moment he heard that he only had three months left to live? To give him his will, that's why."

"Are you now saying that I killed Onorio? It doesn't make sense, Inspector. If he was the only person to know of the existence of a will, I could have seduced him, married him, and then convinced him to destroy it. After a year of marriage, he would have realized that I didn't love him, he would have asked for a divorce, and I would have been free once more. It would have been too easy to get rid of him without resorting to killing him. Onorio was a cold fish, he didn't possess an ounce of passion. He would never have stayed with a wife who neglected him; he would have returned to live in his own home with his old housekeeper."

Samantha was so calm, so sure of herself, that for a moment the inspector believed he had built a castle in the sky. Indeed, her description of Cristaldi was spot on.

"And there's another thing that doesn't make sense," continued the woman, "supposing that there is a will, if

I had destroyed it, Alfonso would never have known that he was entitled to a share of my inheritance. Never in a million years. So why kill him?"

"That's true. But I'm positive I'm right and I'll find out why you killed him," replied the inspector. "In the meantime, I'll ask the judge to free Stefano Baschi. I'm sure he was your sacrificial lamb. It was you who planted the watch at his house to frame him for the murders that you committed."

"Inspector, the news that Stefano Baschi is to be freed gives me great pleasure. He's my best friend, I'm even looking after his cat, aren't I Fufi?" The inspector heard a faint 'meow' that came from somewhere under the sofa. "You'll need a lot more to incriminate me," she continued, "three things. The motive, the opportunity, and the weapon. Point number one, the motive: according to you, the motive is the will, so you will have to prove that it exists or that it existed. Point number two, the opportunity: Cristaldi's housekeeper saw the thief running away from the scene of the crime, and it certainly wasn't me. Point three: where is the weapon?"

"Maybe all I need is the weapon," said Marini, "and to be able to prove that only you, young lady, could have put it in its hiding place."

"Very well. Go and look for it then. Good day."

The inspector left because he didn't have anything more to say. As soon as the door had closed behind him, Samantha let the mask fall from her face, and her beautiful features crumpled in despair.

She picked up the telephone and dialed a number.

"Hello? Is this the office of the notary Angelini? I'd like to make an appointment as soon as possible. Samantha Morelli. Yes... What? Closed for the holidays? Please, I must see him before the holidays, yes, before. When? The day after tomorrow at half past seven? No, no, that time's fine for me. I'll be there at half past seven. Thank you."

April 15th, 2007

Eugenio Morelli knew that there was no hope. After they had taken out his left lung, the right lung continued to fill up with liquid, which had to be drained periodically. Morelli was a doctor, so he knew what was coming: the tumor had metastasized; he could only breath with the help of an oxygen tank. For how much longer, he thought, for how much longer?

His life paraded before his eyes, the best moments and the worst moments. He didn't think he had been a particularly bad man; he had worked to the best of his ability, and loved his family likewise. There was that one occasion when he had cheated on his wife, but he wouldn't call himself an adulterer, no, not if you took account how it happened.

In the summer of 1981, he was at Passignano with his wife and daughter. Samantha was a year old and everyone envied them for their beautiful baby daughter, none more so than the hotelier's wife, a woman of almost forty who didn't have any children of her own. So strong was her desire to have a daughter as beautiful as Samantha that she often took the child from the arms of her mother to hold her and coo over her. The first time this happened Signora Morelli smiled, the second time too, but the third time she took umbrage at the intrusive stranger.

Patrizia Mantegna was a determined person, and one day, finding herself alone with Doctor Morelli in the hotel reception, she said: "Doctor, I need your help."

As he was a plastic surgeon, he ran a professional eye over her face, but saw neither a big nose, nor a cleft lip; the lady was charming.

"What can I do for you?"

"I want a baby, Doctor. As beautiful and as blond as yours. My husband is sterile."

The Doctor smiled regretfully. "I'm sorry, I can't help you there. I specialize in plastic surgery not artificial insemination."

"I'm not asking for artificial insemination. My husband might be infertile, but you sure aren't. You've got a beautiful baby girl to prove it."

Somewhat irritated, Morelli replied: "Why me? Passignano must be full of fertile men!"

"Yes, but it's a small town. Everyone knows everything. Would you rather I had a child with the dentist, or the butcher? Everyone would know. The father has to be a visitor, a tourist."

He continued to refuse, but the poor, desperate woman pleaded with him for days with tears in her eyes, even promising him free board at her hotel for the whole family for ten years. Eventually his compassion for the childless woman got the better of him and he let himself be led into a one of the hotel bedrooms.

The following summer the family returned to the hotel. Signora Mantegna had a son, and Signora Morelli, blissfully unaware of her husband's role in the child's conception, complimented her on her beautiful baby: "I told you it would happen one day! Look what a gorgeous child he his." He had the same blond curls as Samantha, the same that had covered the Doctor's head when he was a child. When he saw those curls, he realized that the child was now his responsibility. His role hadn't ended in the bedroom, the favor he had done for the woman wasn't a simple operation to pin back her ears for free: for heaven's sake, he was now the father of a bastard child. If he had continued to see him, things would have got really complicated which is why, from 1983 until his death, the Morelli family vacationed in the mountains or on the coast, but they never returned to Passignano. Doctor Morelli, however, never stopped thinking about the little blond boy, and as the years passed, he imagined him growing into adulthood. When he discovered he was terminally ill and facing imminent death, Morelli thought it was about time he made amends.

But now, attached to an oxygen tank, and helped by Samantha, he was worried that he had betrayed her. Not wanting her to think badly of him after his death, he decided he had to tell her truth while he could still speak.

And this is why, on April fifteenth, he told her.

"Samantha, as I haven't got long left to live I want you to know what your financial situation will be when I'm dead."

"Papa," she replied, "I know what I'm going to inherit. Don't tire yourself out by speaking."

"No, my dear, there's something that I haven't told you. The villa is yours, and my shares in Unicredit Bank will give you an income of eighty thousand euros a year. You'll be able to live comfortably and pay the taxes on the villa, which are high. You'll also be able to pay for a full time housekeeper."

"I know Papa. And there's another million in the Sella bank. I won't want for anything."

"Actually, I thought that the income from the Unicredit shares would be more than enough to allow you to live without having to work, so I've left the rest of the money to someone else," said Morelli, breathing with difficulty.

Samantha was alarmed. "Don't tease me Papa. I'll be able to live off the money from the Unicredit shares, but I need the money in the other bank to open a publishing house and finance the publication and promotion of all the books I want to publish. You know that's my dream. Anyway, who is this other person?"

"Listen to me, I don't think the publishing house is a good idea. Italians don't like reading. This is why the money in the Sella bank is going to a relative."

"Who? Not that idiot Cousin Franco?"

"No, no, it's a long story. I'm finding it difficult to talk. Listen, my lawyer will tell you."

"Cristaldi? Has he got your will?"

"Yes."

"Have you *really* made a will?" Her tone was so terrible, it was as if she were accusing her father of having committed a crime.

"Yes, my dear. I'm sorry, but I had to."

"You're not leaving the money in the second bank to me? How could you? I'll have to sell the villa if I want to open my publishing house!"

"Samantha, you won't sell anything. Your income will be quite enough to allow you to publish a couple of books, if that's what you really want to do. But don't get your hopes up: you're the daughter of a doctor; you'll never become a famous author. If you really want to be famous, become a politician, or a showgirl. Forget about the publishing house. You won't even sell twenty copies."

"Is that why you're not giving me the money?" she screamed, "Because you don't believe in me?"

"No sweetheart, that's not the reason. I don't believe in Italy. You could be a genius, but the Italian public would never understand."

"You had no right to stop me from trying!"

"Don't upset yourself darling. I just don't want you to be disappointed. You'll still be happy. You're beautiful and you're rich; marry a good man and have lots of wonderful children…"

"I don't want children!" she shouted louder, "I'm not like the other women! I'm twenty-seven years old and my father still doesn't know anything about me! Don't you see? I'm not just another woman!"

"Samantha," pleaded her father, who was very tired.

"Who is this bastard who will get the rest of the money. Who is it?"

"Before I met your mother," lied her father, because it would have taken too long to tell the truth, "I was in a relationship with another woman. And you have a brother. This young man has nothing, and... Do you understand? I had to do what I did."

The girl was silent. She would have been much angrier had her father's objections to her literary ambitions been the only reason why he had decided not to give her the money. But he had another child and any father about to die would have done the same thing.

"Does he know he's my brother?" she asked.

"No, he doesn't."

"Great," murmured Samantha, icily, "I can guarantee that he will never see a cent of that money."

She got up from her chair, and her father saw such hate in her eyes that suddenly he was afraid.

"Samantha, what are you going to do to me?"

She laughed. "What do you think I will do? Block your

oxygen tube? No, Papa. I need you alive for as long as the Lord wants you to suffer on this earth."

No, she didn't want the old man to die immediately, because she needed time.

Time to think. Time to seduce the lawyer, Cristaldi. Time before the will is read.

May 25th, 2007, 6 PM

By now she knew every corner of Onorio's villa. The drawer where he kept his pistol was in his bedroom, the safe was in the study, and in the garden a beautiful magnolia grew up the side of the house and curled around the first floor window. Any fit young lad could have climbed up and entered through the window, but Cristaldi, as he had a gun, wasn't particularly worried. A plan was starting to form in Samantha's head.

"Do you love me?" she had asked him that morning when they were in bed together.

"Of course I love you," he muttered.

"Enough to marry me?"

"I'll have to think about it."

"Why?"

"You're too good in bed. You're incredible. It's obvious that I'm not the first man you've been to bed with."

"You're the second."

"Should I believe you?"

"Why not? You're the second, and you'll be the last if you marry me."

"I'm flattered."

"Would you do anything for me, other than risk your life that is?"

"Anything?" the man smiled. "You women are good

at asking for certain things after sex. It's when men are at their most vulnerable."

"How would you know? I thought I was your first."

They laughed together. "The first in the last fifteen years, yes," replied Cristaldi, "but I too was young, once upon a time."

"So what would you do if... If you were at your most vulnerable?"

"What would you want me to do?"

"The same thing I asked you to do last week but you pretended not to hear me. I want you to destroy my father's will."

"Oh, oh. Now I know why you sleep with me."

She snorted impatiently and said: "But I want to marry you. And you have to destroy that will, for me and for you. Don't you want your wife to be even richer?"

"Sammy, it makes no difference to me. The money that you will inherit is yours, I can't touch it."

"Not every husband thinks like you do."

"I think the way I do because I'm a lawyer. I'm rich too; I don't expect my wife to indulge my whims. If we go on a cruise, I'll pay for the ticket. If I want to buy you something sparkly during our honeymoon, I'll pay the jeweler. What difference does it make to me if you have two million euros or if we have four?"

"Fine. You only want the best for me. But what about my happiness? I want to open a publishing house, but I can't without all of my father's money."

"Yes, you can. Unless you're going to publish books with gold covers studded with diamonds."

"Very funny but that's not why I need the money! If I'm going to be successful, I'm probably going to have to corrupt people."

The lawyer thought for a moment and shook his head. "I'm sorry," he said, "I couldn't possibly defraud a friend."

"Why not?"

Cristaldi had a problem; he didn't know if Morelli had told Samantha about his illegitimate son. Morelli was dead, there was no way of knowing whether he had already told Alfonso that he would be coming into some money: what would happen, if the young man were to come looking for Cristaldi saying, 'my father told me to come and find you'?

Over his long career as a lawyer, Onorio had never once cheated a client, and he had no intention of starting now, not even for Samantha. So he decided lie to her, never once imagining what the consequences would be.

"My dear, up until two weeks ago, I had no idea that this was the reason you sought me out. I really didn't know, and so when your father died, I did my duty and wrote to your brother."

The colour drained from Samantha's face. "What? What letter?"

"I didn't mention money, but you know how these types of letters go. The presence of Alfonso Mantegna is requested at this address on Monday July sixteenth, at six o'clock, as I have some information that may be of interest to him." Actually, the letter was still in Cristaldi's head. He had intended to send it in the next couple of days.

"He's coming on July sixteenth?"

"Yes, and that's why I can't do what you want me to do. Forget about the will."

"You're a bastard," muttered Samantha, who was thinking that not only had she given him her body, she'd also pretended to enjoy giving it. And all for nothing.

"Maybe I am," said Onorio, "and now you're free to

break off the engagement if you wish."

The girl bit her lip with rage and pulled the sheet over her naked body.

"Would you mind giving me a couple of minutes, please?" she asked him.

"Why?"

"If you don't mind, I would like to get dressed without being watched."

Aware of her anger, Onorio smiled bitterly and got out of bed

In the three minutes she was alone, Samantha dressed quickly then took his pistol out of the drawer and slipped it into her bag.

May 25th, 2007, 7 PM

As it was such a warm evening, Samantha had left the house wearing nothing more than a silk top and cotton leggings. Once dressed, she had said a cold goodbye to Onorio and was accompanied by the housekeeper to the gates of the property. She got into her car, a blue Ford, waved goodbye to the housekeeper to be sure that she had been seen, and drove away.

She stopped, however, about twenty-five meters down the road, out of sight of anyone at the villa or the neighboring villas. Then Samantha took a bag from the back seat containing items bought for a few cents at the local market the day before, which, once used, would be carefully dropped into one of the public bins along the street and destroyed by a trash compactor within twenty-four hours.

Inside the bag there was a pair of overalls which were easily slipped on over her flimsy summer clothing, a hat large enough to cover her blond curls, a pair of plimsolls, and a pair of vinyl gloves. Her disguise complete, she got out of the car and walked back up the road carrying a plastic bag, which contained Onorio's gun.

She had never been a frequent visitor to the gym, but she had dabbled in horse riding, which had undoubtedly strengthened her leg and abdominal muscles. It didn't take her long to jump over the villa gates, run through the garden, and climb up the magnolia to the office window.

The lawyer was in there, waiting for his dinner.

"Stay where you are and turn around slowly," said a female voice. Surprised, the lawyer did as he was told and found himself staring into the barrel of a gun.

"Are you mad, sweetheart? Why are you dressed like that?"

"Shut up. I don't know the combination for the safe so you're going to have to open it for me. Open it, quick. You know what you've got to give me."

"No, little girl, I'm not going to give you the will."

"Yes you are, otherwise I'll kill you and your housekeeper will tell everyone that she saw a workman in overalls running off."

It was then that Cristaldi realized that she was serious. Muttering angrily to himself, he started to grapple with the safe, all the while thinking that he could always call the police and report Samantha once she had gone.

"There you are. Take the fucking will and get out of here," he said, throwing the document towards her. The girl picked it up and checked that Eugenio Morelli had actually signed it. Then she dropped it in her bag.

"Don't go thinking you'll get away with it. You know full well that your brother's coming here on the sixteenth of July," said the lawyer, unaware that he had just pronounced not only his own death sentence, but also that of another innocent soul.

"Nobody's coming here," replied Samantha, and then she pulled the trigger. A shot at close range. She couldn't miss.

With his mouth open in shock, he fell, soaking the carpet with his blood, and the girl hurriedly emptied the safe to make it look as though it was a robbery. She didn't leave any fingerprints as she was wearing gloves; her trainers might leave their prints in the garden but they would be in the bin within the hour and crushed before the day was out.

She took the Rolex off the wrist of the victim before leaving, and when the housekeeper burst into the study, the killer was already in the garden.

Thursday, August 9th, 2007

At nine o'clock that evening, Inspector Marini's telephone rang.

He was hoping to receive good news regarding one of his cases, but instead he heard the voice of his girlfriend... hey ho, a friendly voice was better than nothing.

"You seem a bit down," she said.

"I'm really struggling with this case. I can't find anything that could help incriminate Samantha Morelli, but it was her, I'd swear on my mother's life"

"How is the investigation going?"

"I've been in touch with the forensics in Umbria, and they searched the woods at Passignano for evidence to support my theory of a double explosion. I believe she shot her brother with a gun with a silencer and then ran over to the tourists to ask for help, leaving some sort of lit firework in the woods. This would explain the noise the tourists heard when she was already with them."

"The perfect alibi!"

"Right, and I can't disprove it, because there aren't any traces of a firecracker. Not even the odd burnt leaf. And that's not all: when the tourists found Samantha, she was half dressed; she had nowhere to hide a pistol. Where is the weapon? Even supposing she had buried it two meters underground, when did she find the time? Nothing makes sense; the only thing I can think of is that she paid someone to kill him."

"Interesting idea," said Brigida, "she's got the money that's for sure. But how does a little rich girl like her make contact with someone from the underworld?"

"Brigida, you don't know her, and you don't know what she's capable of. It wouldn't surprise me if she had disguised herself as a tramp and gone and recruited one of the addicts who smoke joints under the arches. There are many people in Rome who are so desperate for drugs that they would kill their own mother for five thousand euros."

"If you're right," said Brigida, "the murder weapon could still be in the possession of the killer."

"Exactly, and that's why we'll never find it," said Marini, flatly.

"What are you going to do?"

"I don't know. In the meantime, I've asked the judge to let poor Baschi out of prison. He'll be out tomorrow, and he hasn't got any relatives so I'll pick him up and take him home: once we get chatting, he could tell me something interesting about Samantha."

"A ride for a chat, eh?" Brigida laughed. "Nothing in life is ever free."

June 30th, 2007

On the island boat, Samantha turned her face towards the breeze and breathed in; not a curl was out of place. Alfonso smiled at her.

"Where are you from?" he asked.

"Rome."

"The centre of the city?"

"I live in Olgiata."

"So you're rich then."

"Can't complain. Do you know Olgiata? Have you ever been to Rome?"

"No."

"Really? You've never seen our capital city?"

"I haven't had time."

It was time to ask that all-important question.

"Are you thinking of going soon? Every Italian must see their capital city!"

"I'm still young; I'll go one day."

Not the sixteenth of July then, thought Samantha.

"If you organized a trip to Rome this summer, you could stay at my villa. I've got loads of free rooms. What do you think?"

"It's a fantastic offer," he replied, "but I can't leave Passignano in the summer. I've got to work. If you're serious, I could come in October."

Crap, thought Samantha, what the hell has happened to Cristaldi's letter? Hasn't he received it?

No, hang on a second. What if he has got the letter, but doesn't want Signor Mantegna to know that he's not his son? If I were him, I wouldn't want anyone to know either. I wouldn't want to embarrass Signor and Signora Mantegna.

As you wish, Alfonso. Hide the letter if you must.

Friday, August 10th, 2007, 9 AM

Stefano Baschi found the Inspector Marini waiting for him when he came into the room to receive his personal belongings that had been taken from him when he was arrested.

"Oh!" he said, surprised, "Good morning, Inspector. What are you doing here?"

"I wanted to offer you a lift home seeing that you won't be receiving any damages for wrongful arrest, or anyway, not immediately. A lift is the least I can do."

"That's very kind of you, thank you," said the young man, coldly, and went up to the desk where a plastic bag full of his belongings was waiting for him.

"I'm now going to read you a list of what's inside the bag," said the policeman behind the desk, "please check that the objects on the list correspond with the objects in the bag and sign this receipt."

"Fine"

"A Swiss Laurens wristwatch with a black leather strap, a brown leather belt ninety centimeters long. A pack of tissues, a pack of sugar-free chewing gum, a black leather wallet containing twelve euros and forty cents, a Visa card and a used train ticket."

"It's all there," said Stefano, hoping that the inspector wasn't listening, but Marini was right behind him.

"What do you mean, a used train ticket?" he asked the policeman.

"That's what's written on the list, Signore."

"Can I see it please?"

"But sir —"

"Sir, my ass! I'm a police inspector for heaven's sake. I was the one with a search warrant for this young man's house. I'm authorized by fucking law to see his wallet!"

Stefano Baschi paled. The policeman gave the wallet to the inspector who looked at the train ticket.

Ticket: Rome-Perugia, Perugia-Rome.

"Holy shit!" he cried, "we searched his house, but nobody thought to check what he had on him! The most important piece of evidence was in his wallet!"

"What evidence, Inspector?" asked Stefano.

Marini glared at him. "I promised to give you a lift home, and I will. But I need you to tell me why," he picked up the ticket, and waved it under the young man's nose, "you have this in your possession."

Friday, August 10th, 9:30 AM

Once inside the car, Marini spoke frankly.

"Now young man, we're here in my car without witnesses or microphones. Everything you say will remain between you and me. You have two choices: the first is telling me why you have this train ticket, and in doing so, help me send Samantha to prison, and the second is not telling me anything. If you choose the second, I'll have you back in prison within twenty-four fucking hours."

Stefano stared at the dashboard in silence.

"Did you hear what I said?"

"Yes. I don't care if you do send me back to prison, and anyway you haven't got a single shred of evidence against Samantha," said Stefano.

"You don't care about yourself, eh? Fine, tell me about this ticket. It's dated July eighth, the day of the second murder. You were in Passignano."

"I was in Perugia, Inspector. There's no mention of Passignano."

"Don't get clever with me boy, otherwise I swear to God, I'll break all the fucking bones in your body. Go ahead and report me; I don't care. Now, I'm going to ask you one more time: why have you got this train ticket?"

Stefano gave a wry smile. "Because I'm an idiot," he said eventually. "I knew full well I should have thrown it away when I arrived in Rome, and I forgot."

"Now we're getting somewhere. Did you kill Alfonso Mantegna?"

"Yes."

"Did Samantha pay you to do it?"

"Nobody paid me."

"Are we back to playing stupid games again?"

"Inspector, I would never accept money from a woman I loved. I knew that Alfonso's death would have helped her, and that's why I decided to kill him."

"So it was all your idea, eh?"

Stefano didn't reply. Suddenly the inspector slapped him.

"Owww!"

"I warned you about lying to me. This is a friendly chat, off the record, and when the time comes you could deny ever having spoken to me. But today I want the truth. You're right, I don't have any proof that it was Samantha, and I won't be able to use your words as evidence against her. It's to satisfy my own personal curiosity, okay?"

Stefano thought for a moment. No microphones, no witnesses. He could deny everything.

"Fine. Samantha asked me to do what I did, but I didn't ask her for money. What else do you want to know?"

"First of all, tell me why nobody saw you at the station."

The young man smiled. "Not even my mother would have recognized me had she been alive. I was wearing a Hawaiian shirt, flowery shorts, dark glasses, and my hair was slicked back with gel."

"Disguised as a hippy! Son of a bitch!"

"It was Samantha's idea. She's the clever one," continued Stefano, proud to be able to talk about his woman now that she was beyond the arm of the law. "She planned two murders that were to be committed with the same weapon, but by two different people. She knew it would drive the police crazy. You would never have guessed if it hadn't been for that damned ticket."

"So you're proud of yourselves, are you? Very well, now tell me the whole story, starting from the beginning."

"In the middle of June, Samantha came to my house and asked me if I would do something dangerous for her That could well have been the day she hid Cristaldi's watch in my drawer. I didn't kill him."

"I believe you. That's why you were so shocked when we found the watch. Samantha had planned the perfect crime for you in Passignano; she swore to you that nobody would ever find out, which is why you didn't expect her to frame you for another murder! Isn't that what happened? Now I understand what you meant when you said 'Samantha wants me in prison,' but then you took it back. Why Stefano? Why didn't you tell us that only Samantha could have put that watch there?"

Stefano shook his head without saying anything.

"To be in love is something, to be an idiot is something else entirely," muttered the inspector. "Come on, I want to hear the rest of the story."

"Samantha came to me, told me her plans, and then

she left. She was traveling by car, her blue Ford. Once in Passignano, it was easy to find her," he interrupted himself. He didn't want to give the inspector information that he hadn't been aware of.

"Her brother," replied Marini, "I know all about the will. You can continue."

Stefano nodded. "She had read the will before burning it and so knew the guy's name and surname. She reeled him in and arranged to meet him in the woods and then, the day before the meeting she called me. She used a phone box so no one could trace her calls, and all she said was: come on the train tomorrow morning. I did what she asked. She was going to meet Alfonso in the afternoon, so at midday Samantha and I started to explore the woods. She had found a sort of sharp drop, it that's the right name for it, anyway, an area in the woods where you can see the main road. The drop was covered with dry leaves so it was easy for someone to slide down and reach the main road without a scratch. To climb back up would be impossible, but sliding down was child's play, and you always ended up at the same point, virtually on top of a milestone. Samantha left her car next to this stone as that day she wouldn't need it. The woods are near the hotel, less than a mile away; a breeze for someone used to walking like Samantha is. She gave me the keys to the Ford, obviously she had another set, and she also gave me the pistol, and all this, before lunch."

By now the inspector had understood everything. He sighed. "Yes, continue."

"At half past four, Samantha took Alfonso to the woods. They rolled around a bit and he opened his trousers but just as he was getting into it, she said she had to nip off for a wee, and left him alone. He lay on the dry leaves and waited for her, while I waited behind a tree and I didn't move until I heard Samantha shout 'help!' She had told me to be very careful at this point: if she shouted help, it meant that she had met other people, and as soon as she met them, her alibi would be in place. So I waited until Samantha had her alibi, then I left my hiding place and shot that poor man. Everybody heard the shot, but it was useless looking for me: I'd thrown myself down the dip, slipping down on the dry leaves, and I arrived pretty much next to Samantha's car. I got in, and off I went. I drove as quickly as I could to the station at Perugia, parked the car where Samantha had told me to, and took the next train home. She told me to leave the pistol in the car under the passenger seat."

"Brilliant!" commented the inspector.

"I know. Samantha had planned everything carefully; she was also sure that she would meet someone in the woods that day. She pretended to be terrified and was taken back to her hotel. Then, at dinnertime, she told everyone that she was popping out for a breath of fresh air to calm her nerves, left the hotel on foot, and got the last coach to Perugia."

Marini nodded. "She went to the station, picked up her car with the pistol inside, and took it back to Passignano."

"Exactly."

"Stefano, where is the pistol?"

"I don't know. Samantha told me she would clean my fingerprints off it but that it was an unnecessary precaution as no one would ever find it."

"Unnecessary? I imagine it was, seeing that she meant to frame you for Cristaldi's murder."

Yet again, Stefano refused to say anything.

"How could you love a woman like that?" said the inspector suddenly.

"It's no use trying to explain it to you because you're only judging her on what she's done over the last three months, but I've known her for fifteen years."

"Fair enough. She's beautiful, intelligent, she's got class. But is that enough to make you fall in love with a person who kills in cold blood, for money, and who has transformed a good person like yourself into an assassin?"

"For money? No. If anything, it was to save her future. For the love of her publishing house. It was her only dream, Inspector. Samantha's mother died of leukemia when Samantha was only seven years old, leaving her alone with a despotic father who tried to stifle her literary ambitions. There's nothing worse for an artist to hear the words 'forget about art'. Dr Morelli would never accept that Samantha was a genius; all he wanted was a son in law and grandchildren. She doesn't have an easy life; the men she meets either want to marry her for her money, or sleep with her because she is beautiful, but nobody is interested in what she can do and Samantha writes beautifully. I'm the only one who loves what she writes, I read her books; I encourage her. So when her father tried to deny her the money she needed to open a publishing house, something inside Samantha's head snapped. But I was the only one she trusted enough to come to for help."

"Listen, kid, ninety per cent of the population has a difficult life, but ninety per cent of the population is not made up of assassins. A difficult life doesn't justify murder."

"Artists aren't like normal people. They live in their own little world, and if you take them out of their world, it sends them crazy."

"You can say whatever you like Stefano, but I'm not going to agree with you."

"Let me tell you something." said the young man. "When I decided not to live with my aunts anymore, I went to live alone and adopted a cat. Samantha said that I had the right to choose an animal to alleviate my solitude, but to remember that I was violating the rights of the cat. The poor creature would have been much happier in a garden than in an tiny three-roomed apartment on the seventh floor."

"Are you really telling me that I have to believe she has a noble and sensitive soul just because she likes animals?"

"No Inspector, I'm trying to tell you that Samantha is the only person in the world who is capable of writing a poem on such a delicate subject."

"A poem?"

"I know it off by heart. Do you want to hear it?" Marini didn't reply, so Stefano, his voice full of emotion, started to recite:

"I saved a little kitten,
Orphaned, minuscular,
Destined to die
Under the sun.
Bewitched by the light
Of two little stars,
I took him home.
Now
A soft adult,
A companion
In my solitude.
Your eyes
Full of wisdom.
Maybe you know

Of a world out there
Beyond my house,
Beyond my silence,
Sense a universe
Denied
You are silent.
And every evening,
I stroke your velvet fur
And ask forgiveness
For having saved you."

The inspector was silent for a few moments. The sadness of the poem had managed to reach that tiny part of his hardened soul that was still vulnerable to emotions. Obviously, those verses sprang from the same small part of Samantha's soul.

"Incredible!" is all he could say.

"Do you feel it, Inspector? Do you feel it too? Samantha manages to capture the pain that comes from the smallest things, and she does the same in her novels."

"So why then is she capable of killing human beings? Doesn't she feel the pain of her victims?"

"She feels it but she projects it into another dimension. Inspector, an artist only absorbs those emotions that can be used to create art: only those. All the other emotions slide off here. This is why there is a big difference between the emotions a writer feels in life, and those which they express in their writing."

"You sound as if you've dedicated your life to psychoanalysis!"

"But I have, yes, to be able to understand the woman I loved."

"So what you're telling me is there is nothing in this

world that you wouldn't do for her. She asked you to kill someone and you did. How was she going to repay you, if not with money?"

"What do you mean 'repay me'?"

"Did you think she would marry you, or was there something else?"

Stefano shook his head. "I'm under no illusions. Samantha will never marry: she spends twelve hours a day writing or studying."

Marini sighed. "I think you're as insane as your precious writer. However, you've earned your ride."

He started the engine and the car moved off. Neither spoke during the journey.

It was only once they'd reached Stefano's house that the inspector said: "Wait a minute. There's something that doesn't make sense. Cristaldi's murder was disguised as robbery; Alfonso's death was blamed on a mad man who stalked couples. Samantha could have stopped there. Why then did she invent the story of the disappointed suitor who killed her fiancés?"

"Inspector, don't underestimate the press. Sooner or later, a nosy journalist would have started poking around, written a piece about the rich heiress who brought bad luck to her boyfriends....and the police would have linked the murder in Rome with the one in Passignano and interrogated Samantha. To come up with the story about the disappointed suitor two months after Alfonso's murder would have been dangerous; better to mention it now rather than later."

Marini nodded in agreement. "But Samantha could have stopped there, the investigations wouldn't have come to anything without the famous watch. Why did she leave the watch in your house? I've been asking you this question all day, Stefano. She wanted you to go to prison: was that how she was going to repay you for having loved and protected her?"

"I've got an idea," said Stefano, "but I fear it's so stupid, you'll never believe me. So I've decided not to say anything."

The Inspector opened the car door. "Get out, you poor, stupid boy," he said, "and enjoy your freedom because it won't last long. I'll be back once I've got the murder weapon, and until then I'll be keeping this train ticket safe."

Monday, August 13th, 2007

"You will never find the murder weapon."

Her words troubled Inspector Marini, but by now he knew that Samantha had retrieved the gun a couple of hours after Alfonso's death, and he was certain that it was still at Passignano. As it wasn't in the woods, it could have been thrown into the lake sometime between the morning of July ninth and the evening of the eleventh, which was when the girl returned to Rome.

So Marini went back to Passignano and asked the authorities there if the lake could be searched. The operation was expensive, but as Marini had in his possession an order signed by a judge, the police force in Perugia were in no position to complain.

While the divers were doing their job, Inspector Marini went to see Signor Mantegna to inform him of the latest developments in the case.

"We believe that the motive for the murder is the inheritance from Doctor Morelli," he said, "so we presume that Alfonso knew that he would have inherited something from the Doctor. I would be grateful if you could have a look through Alfonso's belongings for a letter from Rome."

"A letter from Rome?" repeated Mantegna, perplexed.

"Yes, from Doctor Morelli, or from a lawyer called Cristaldi."

The old man shook his head. His eyes glistened with tears.

"Alfonso died for nothing," he said, "I would never have let him accept a cent of that inheritance. I'm still alive, and officially the boy was my son! I would have forced him to refuse the money."

The Inspector was silent: he respected the father's pain and didn't dare to say what he was really thinking, which was: *"Signor Mantegna, you told me that you didn't know Alfonso very well. Are you sure that he would have refused an enormous amount of money just to please you?"*

"If that woman killed him for money," continued the old man, his voice full of hate, "she must pay. It doesn't matter whether he was my blood or not, he was my life, and now I've got nothing!"

"I understand, Signor Mantegna." Inspector Marini couldn't wait to leave, but as the man so obviously needed someone to talk to, he felt he had to wait for him to continue.

"If I had known that the young lady was putting on an act, an obscene act, I wouldn't have let her stay for the funeral, I would have kicked her out of the church. And with that cushion too, what was I thinking!"

"Cushion?"

"A silk cushion with my son's initials embroidered on one side, A.M., one last twist of the knife: what did they stand for? Alfonso Mantegna or Alfonso Morelli?"

The inspector started. He felt a strange sensation run up his spine, but this time it wasn't nausea, it was something much more pleasurable. "Wait a minute, Signor Mantegna, where is that cushion now?"

"Where do you think? Under my son's head."

"Underground."

The two men stared at one another, but the old man didn't understand what the inspector was getting at.

"How big was it?" continued Marini.

"A bit smaller than a normal pillow. Does it matter?"

"Could it be opened? Did it have buttons down the side?"

"I don't know. I didn't really look at it. Samantha put it in the coffin with her own hands."

"With her own hands?" shouted the inspector, and punched the table.

"What's going on?" asked the old man, shocked.

"I'm really sorry to make things harder for you, Signor Mantegna, but we're going to have to exhume Alfonso's corpse."

Thursday, August 16th, 2007

The inspector wasn't in the least surprised to see Stefano Baschi seated in Samantha's sitting room; by now he knew it was wrong to think that the poor disappointed suitor would not be allowed in the villa.

"Are you both here?" said Marini, coming into the room with a young policewoman. "Great. You've saved me a trip. I've got two arrest warrants here, and if the young man weren't here I would have had to arrest him at his house."

Samantha raised an eyebrow but didn't reply; she was waiting to hear the evidence against her.

"Agent Fortunelli," continued the inspector, pointing at the young policewoman, "has got two cats, and she'll be looking after yours. I could never have abandoned it after hearing that poem."

Samantha looked questioningly at Stefano, who couldn't help smiling despite the seriousness of the situation.

"What evidence have you got against us?" asked the girl.

"I haven't got your father's will, I haven't got eyewitnesses to the crime, and I haven't got fingerprints! But I have got an ivory coloured silk pillow with a pistol hidden inside."

Samantha went white and said no more. It was only then that Stefano understood how Samantha had got rid of the pistol: she had been true to the principal 'if one head organises everything, the less the accomplices know the better.'

"Madam," said Marini, "do you remember what I said to you last time I was here?" Two men were killed by two bullets shot from the same pistol. Finding the murder weapon wouldn't be enough to identify the killer, but if I could prove that only one person, only one, could have put the weapon in the place where it was found, then it's game over for the killer. You put that silk cushion under Alfonso Mantegna's head just before the coffin was closed; we've got at least ten witnesses, all Alfonso's relatives and friends who were asking themselves 'who is that blond' and didn't take their eyes off you."

Samantha nodded, conceding victory to the inspector.

"You'd do well to remain silent. You do know your

rights, don't you? You have the right to remain silent until you have appointed a defense lawyer, and once he is present, we'll start the official interrogation. You are accused of first degree murder of the lawyer Onorio Cristaldi and instigating the murder of Alfonso Mantegna. I really do hope that you are jailed for life. Your friend here was psychologically pressured into committing murder, and I'll be giving evidence to that effect in court. I hope that the judge will take into account the extenuating circumstances and he'll get away with a prison term of no more than fourteen years, reduced for good behavior."

At last Samantha spoke. "I'm happy that you want to help Stefano. At this point I could have admitted to both murders, but no judge would have believed me considering that there are those witnesses that heard the shot in Passignano."

"Exactly, said the inspector, "and now we have to go."

"Am I allowed to go upstairs to get a change of underwear?" asked the girl.

"Yes, but no more than two or three pieces, and Agent Fortunelli will go with you."

When the two women came back downstairs, the inspector looked at Stefano's anguished face and took pity on him.

"I don't think you'll be able to see one another before the trial. You can say goodbye now if you wish."

Samantha thanked him with a smile. She went up to Stefano, kissed him on the cheek, and said: "I'm so sorry. Forgive me. For everything."

As she was speaking, she took his hands in hers and Stefano felt her pushing a tiny object between his fingers.

"Let's go." said the inspector and took Stefano by the

arm, while the policewoman took Samantha away. Stefano didn't dare look at what Samantha had given him as she said her goodbyes, but he guessed what it was by its shape and burst into tears, sobbing: "No! Samantha, no!"

Marini didn't ask why.

Monday, August 20th, 2007

"There's a visitor for you." Stefano walked into the visitor's room at the Regina Coeli prison and found the inspector waiting for him. Who else could it have been? He didn't have any relatives other than the aunts who had brought him up, and they wanted nothing more to do with their nephew the murderer.

"Good morning, Inspector." said the young man. "Any news?"

"Yes, I came to tell you that your cat has been adopted. His new family have a house with a garden."

"Good. Samantha will be pleased too," said Stefano. "She fought for the right of every cat to have a garden."

The inspector stared hard at his hands.

"She's dead, isn't she," muttered the prisoner.

The other man winced. "Who told you?"

"No one. But you didn't come here to talk about my cat. Samantha managed to communicate her intentions to kill herself to me."

"Was that before the arrest?"

"No. As we were being arrested, she put a tablet into my hand. I knew then that I would never see her again."

"Christ!" exclaimed Marini. "You were crying for her death that day! Why didn't you warn me? We could have saved her."

"No," said Stefano, shaking his head. "She wasn't the

kind of woman you could keep in a cage with a prostitute who sells her body for twenty euros, or a drug pusher, or an illiterate housewife who killed her abusive husband. Samantha would never have tolerated those kind of people."

"I know," said the inspector, "as soon as she arrived, she asked to be put in isolation, but the head of the prison refused, so during the night Samantha tried to strangle a prisoner while she slept. After that they had to put her in isolation and she was happy. She needed to be alone for a night. Do you want to know what she did?"

Stefano nodded.

"She took off her panties and ripped the seams with her teeth. There must have been at least twenty tablets sewn into the lining. She swallowed them with some water, put her underwear back on and lay down on her bunk. The next morning, they found her dead, but they were at a loss to know what had happened. If it weren't for the ripped panties and the results of the autopsy. She had swallowed an extremely high dose of beta-blockers which caused a heart attack. Your woman really was a criminal genius."

"Yes, Samantha's father took beta-blockers. She must have had a supply at home. Who knows how long she had them sewed in the lining, it's not something she could have done the day we were arrested, although I do remember that she asked to go upstairs to get something," Stefano agreed.

"She did," confirmed the inspector. "I'm pretty sure she was ready from the day I told her that she was under suspicion. She must have decided there and then that should she be arrested, she would kill herself. She'd even made a will; I found out yesterday when her notary called me."

"Samantha never left anything to chance," said Stefano, with the air of a proud father.

"Do you know who will inherit her estate?"

"No, I don't. Other than a cousin whom she hated, she didn't have any relatives."

"It's odd she never said anything because you're her only heir."

The prisoner started in surprise. "That's impossible. It's illegal, isn't it?"

"The law stops a convicted murderer from accepting an inheritance, but not an accomplice. The will is legal."

"Oh my God, so I'm..." the young man's eyes widened as though he could see a future full of endless possibilities.

"Now then, boy," said Marini, "when you get out of here, you'll be forty years old with a fantastic villa and three million euros, plus the interest accrued. Samantha has offered you a new life in exchange for the one she took away from you. A guilty conscience works wonders."

Stefano shook his head. "A guilty conscience? No, Inspector, it's an act of love and I know how I'll repay it. I will open the publishing house that Samantha dreamed of, and I'll publish the books she wrote; I know where she keeps them. Actually, you know what? It'll be even easier to convince the public to buy them, because now the author is a famous female assassin. People are bloodthirsty: they'll be reading them, expecting all sorts of blood and guts and stuff when in fact Samantha wrote beautiful books."

"Stefano!" shouted the inspector, shocked by this frenzied outburst of emotion, but the young man wasn't listening.

"She's done it! She wanted to be a famous writer, and

to get what she wanted she had to become a killer and then kill herself! For the love of God! She's done it! I'll publish her books, I will!"

Marini was baffled.

"Stefano, are you aware of what you are saying?"

"Is there something wrong? Inspector, don't you remember what I told you about artists? The artist, if their world is threatened, will kill, but if their world is destroyed, the artist dies. When Samantha swallowed the pills, inside she was already dead. I had to accept her wishes. But through her books she will be immortal."

"Enough of this rubbish! She was the one who sent you to prison, and now you want to dedicate the rest of your life rendering her immortal through her books? Wouldn't you rather forget all about her, free yourself from an obsession that has enslaved you, and start again? If I were in your position, I would take the money, go to Australia, and become a sheep farmer. Anything to forget Samantha!"

Stefano shook his head. "All my life I loved her, and she loved me. There's nothing left to say."

"Oh! She loved you? That's news to me. So it was for love that she left Onorio Cristaldi's watch in your apartment, was it?"

"Yes, it was."

"You're a fool, boy, completely mad. You'd do well to carry on like this in court, they'll lock you up in a secure unit for the mentally unstable, oh yes, boy, mentally unstable. You'll get three years in a hospital, then you'll be free to go off and publish Samantha's books! I don't know why it's taken me so long to realize that you are completely insane. Goodbye."

"She loved me!" cried Stefano, with tears in his eyes.

"Now I'm sure. I knew before but her will proves it! I'm the only man she ever loved!"

"Poor devil," muttered the inspector as he left the room.

April 25th, 2002

In Stefano's bed, Samantha wound a corner of the sheet around her fingers, lost in thought. Her silence worried the young man.

"Darling, are you alright?"

"Yes."

"Did I hurt you?"

"No, it was nothing."

"I'm sorry. I didn't realize it was your first time. Why should I. You're twenty two years old and the most courted lady in Italy for Christ's sake!"

"Yes, but you've known me since I was a child. You know sex doesn't interest me."

"Why did we do it then?"

"Because I love you. Aren't you happy to be the first?"

Calmed by her words, Stefano moved closer to her in the bed, but Samantha pulled away.

"Wait," she said, "Remember that I love you because I won't tell you ever again, not tomorrow, not next year, never."

"Why not?"

"Because my feelings for you are *my* problem Stefano, and only mine. I can't marry you, I can't have children with you, and I can't spend the rest of my life with you."

"Why, my darling?" he asked, sweetly.

"Don't you know? Don't you know what I want from life? I love you so much that I would spend all of my time talking to you, walking with you, or holding you. I might not have any time to write, and at first I won't care. But what happens when I'm sixty years old, Stefano? When I'm sixty years old, I'll look back at my life and say: what have I done? I haven't become a famous writer, and whose fault is that? Yours, my dear, and I would hate you. It would be awful if we were to hate one another when we are old."

He nodded because he understood. "What do you suggest we do then?" he asked, ready to do anything for her.

"Remain friends. Do you want to be my best friend forever? You can marry someone else, if you want to be a father, but you won't have to stop seeing me."

"I don't want another woman. I'm just happy to have your company, that is when you are free to give it to me," replied Stefano.

"It's a deal."

This time he was on top of her. He kissed her neck, and she abandoned herself to him with all the passion that she was capable of. In those brief moments, Samantha understood that her alter ego was the same as all the other women; she understood that she would have to deny herself this pleasure forever. It was a disconcerting thought.

"Stefano..."

"Yes, my love?"

"Forgive me. But maybe one day I'll have to rid myself of you."

"What do you mean?"

"I don't know. You being in my life jeopardizes everything that I want to become. What I feel for you scares me. What would you do if one day, in a moment of insanity, I tried to shut you out of my life?"

Stefano looked at her in the eyes and once again he understood her tormented soul.

"I would forgive you, darling," he replied, "I'll always forgive you."

The Price of Revenge

On a damp, rainy day in Palermo in early March 2007, Flora Persici gave a sigh of relief and started to clean the paint off her hands. The painting was finally finished.

Behind her, Flavio murmured.

"It's fantastic," he said. "What are you going to call it?"

"The Footpath," she replied.

"Wouldn't 'The Endless Trail' be better?"

"It's up to the public to understand that the path's not going anywhere."

"I guess you're right."

It was a picture of a raggedy old lady leaning on her stick as she walked down a country lane. The lane was lined with trees that curved their twisted branches around her as though they were about to reach in and grab her. On the tips of the branches she had painted the most grotesque nails. In the background, on the left, there was a ruined hovel but the lane turned to the right, suggesting that the old lady would never reach her destination: was she heading towards her death? Flora wanted the viewers of her painting to be tormented by the same anguish as that caused by Munch's Scream.

Flavio put his hands on the painter's shoulders and gently kissed her neck.

"I'm so happy," he said.

"Why?"

"Because not only is my woman the sexiest woman in the world, she's also a genius. What more could life give me?"

Smiling, Flora closed her eyes and let him kiss her. She was tall and slim, blond, with the most splendid green eyes; quite possibly her lack of curves would have stopped her from winning a beauty contest, but there was no doubt that she was sexy. She had the sensuality of so many artists that comes from the aura of spirit and refinement that surrounds them. Flavio was her ideal companion, he was handsome and just as sensitive when it came to art as she was — an architect.

They met at high school, and stayed together despite their paths separating when she went to art school and he to university; they were two halves of the same soul. They had been in love since they were fifteen years old, but had only moved into together once they had reached a certain level of economic security which came when they were both twenty-eight. They had now been living together for three years and both were of the opinion that they should never have children so that they could dedicate all their time to art.

"Shall we celebrate the completion of the painting?" he whispered in her ear.

"How?"

"How about going to the movies this evening?"

"Is there anything good on?"

"Woody Allen's latest." Their words were punctuated by kisses.

"It'll be the usual story of a horny bastard who sees his therapist once a week." Flora didn't like Woody Allen.

"But it'll be funny."

"Fine. Woody Allen it is then. After dinner?"

"Why not, as long as there's something worth eating in this house."

"The fridge is bursting at the seams."

"Great. I'm off to have a shower."

"No, I'll go first. I'm covered in paint."

"We'll have a shower together then."

"Pervert," murmured Flora, but she was smiling. It certainly wouldn't be the first time that they had scrubbed each other's backs...

* * *

It was half past ten when they came out of the cinema. Flora looked around her; only one flickering streetlight illuminated the dark street.

"This place is a dump! The next time you invite me to the cinema, don't bring me to such an awful neighbourhood, okay?"

"In my defence, it was the only cinema that was showing the film, but I promise we won't come here again."

"And no more Woody Allen. I didn't even laugh once."

Flora's character was as fiery as Flavio's was mild, so they never argued. Their odd squabble was nothing when compared to the passion that united them; when Flavio had started his own architectural practice, the first thing he did was to design a villa that would become their love nest, and he built it for her. All her whims and desires were incorporated into his drawings: a large, bright room for painting in, a smaller room where the paintings would be left to dry, a pretty garden with a lawn....he had even signed the title deeds over to her. An old aunt had left her a cottage in the country, perfect for escaping summer in the city, but the lovers liked their villa so much that they only stayed there from the fifth to the twenty-fifth of August, when the closure of the shops in the city left them no choice but to seek refuge in an area frequented by tourists. She was indulged in every way and was enormously grateful to her man.

"Where's your car? I can't see a thing."

"I know exactly where we are. It's over there. Come on."

They had almost reached the car when two thugs came out of nowhere and blocked the street in front of them. They had spiky hair and a dozen piercings in their ears and noses; it was quite obvious what they were after. One was thin and wiry, the other stocky and plump.

"Hey, you!" said the thin one to Flavio. "Get your wallet out!"

Flavio tossed it in his direction without a word: it wasn't worth arguing over a bit of money. He wisely didn't keep his documents in his wallet, only the cash he needed for a night at the cinema; he had given the cashier at the cinema a fifty-euro note and received thirty-six euros in change. Before letting them go however, the thieves started counting the money.

"Thirty-six euros?" sneered the first one. "Do you expect me to believe that a man dressed like you, with a hot babe like her, has only got thirty six euros in his wallet? Who do you think you're kidding? Where's the rest?"

"That's all I've got," said Flavio, "and please be aware that the 'hot babe' here is my wife and we've been to the cinema. How much money do you think you need to buy two cinema tickets, you bastard?"

The thug didn't much care for his reply and turned to his accomplice.

"Carlo, I think someone needs their manners seen to. He called me a bastard."

Carlo grabbed Flavio and slammed him against the hood of the car.

"No!" screamed Flora. "Leave him alone!"

"Be quiet, whore, otherwise Carlo will be forced to teach *you* a lesson too."

Flora wasn't the type of girl who ran away at the first sight of trouble. Both the thugs were now hitting Flavio and she tried to pull one of them away, but she was pushed back with such force that she was knocked to the ground.

"Leave him alone!" she shouted again as she was getting up. "We've got a car. Here, take the keys to the car!"

"We don't steal cars, that's not our thing," replied the thin one. "Money or nothing. How much cash have you got?"

Flora started rooting desperately in her bag but all she could find was twelve euros. The thieves would have thought she was mocking them if she had offered them such a derisory amount, and that would have made things worse. She let her bag fall to the ground and threw herself back into the throng, but this time she was hit so hard that her nose started to bleed.

Sat on the ground, shocked, she stared at the blood that rolled down her fingers; she only realised that Flavio was lying on the floor motionless, when she felt the eyes of the thugs on her.

"What have we here?" said the thin one. "She really is a pretty little thing. A nice piece of ass. Shall we have a bit of fun before we go?"

"Shit yeh. Why not?" said the other one but at that moment came the distance sound of a police siren and a flashing blue light lit up the night sky.

"Go!" said one of the thugs, and they both disappeared into the darkness. The next minute two policemen were helping Flora up.

"What happened? Have you been attacked?"

"No. My boyfriend is over there. He's been beaten up pretty badly."

The policemen immediately called for another patrol car to follow the thieves, and then turned their attention to the injured.

One went up to Flavio while the other one examined

the woman.

"Let's have a look at that nose. No it's not broken. There'll be no lasting damage to your beauty, madam. Anyway, we'll call an ambulance just to be on the safe side."

But before he could reach for his radio, the second policeman turned towards him.

"Marco! Get over here.The young man's unresponsive. I think he's dead."

"Dead?" stammered Flora. The policeman gently lent her against the hood of the police car and tried to reassure her.

"My colleague is probably exaggerating. Don't worry, Miss, I'll go and have a look.Wait for me here."

Flora wanted to run over to where her fiancé was lying; she wanted to see how he was for herself, but her legs had started tremble and refused to do what they were being told to by her brain. Nervous shock. She had to stay where she was, propped up against the police car to stop herself from falling, but that didn't stop her from hearing the voices of the policemen in the distance.

"Christ! He really *is* dead. They've split his skull open. Look."

Flora fell to the ground, unconscious.

* * *

When she came round, she found herself sprawled on a comfortable sofa at the police station.

"Madam," a female voice was saying, "Madam, can you hear me?"

"Yes." The clouds before her eyes cleared just enough for her to be able to make out the large, good-natured face of a female police officer.

"Where's Flavio?" asked Flora.

There was no reply. She tried to get up from the sofa, but was pushed roughly back down.

"Where is Flavio?" she shouted again.

"I'm sorry my dear. You can't see him at the moment."

"Christ! He really is dead." That's what she'd heard before she fainted.

"Did they beat him to death? Please tell me. Have they killed him?"

The policewoman sighed and nodded; steeling herself for an outbreak of hysterics from the girl, but Flora forced herself to remain calm.

"Did they have a weapon?" she murmured.

"No. They slammed his head against the ground until he was dead. We don't know what the motive was for the attack. Do you know why they chose you?"

"They robbed us," replied the painter, "and we didn't have enough money." She felt as though she was in a trance, and that the words coming out of her belonged to someone else. It wasn't possible that Flavio was dead and she was here, able to answer the questions put to her by the policewoman. It wasn't possible that her past and her future life had been destroyed and she had survived. Obviously she was in the afterlife and someone else was talking through her body....

"Are you telling me that they took your wallet and then they attacked you because they wanted more money?"

"Yes."

"How terrible. One of our patrol cars followed them, but they had already disappeared. Could you describe them to me?"

"Describe them?" murmured the woman who was in Flora's body. "I can do better than that. I'm a painter and if you give me a piece of paper and a pen, I'll be able to draw them for you."

"Could you do that?"

"Yes."

Flavio is dead. Dead. I'll go home and he won't be there. I'll paint the next picture and there won't be anybody behind me who will say: 'it's fantastic'. The villa is still there, built by him for me, and every corner echoes with our love, and he isn't there. He'll never be there. I have loved him since I was fifteen years old. How will I be able to live without Flavio? How will I be able —?

"Madam," said the policewoman, "I think you are suffering from shock. Before we go any further, I would like you to see a doctor. Madam? Can you hear me?"

But Flora had fainted again.

* * *

Fifteen days later she was released from hospital. When she got the keys to the villa back, she held them tightly in her hand and felt her stomach turn over. She didn't want to go back to that house that was so full of memories, so full of him.

But she didn't have anywhere else to go other than the cottage in the country, and it was still too cold. No. She had to face up to her new life without Flavio, although not immediately, she didn't have to start it immediately.... and that is why, instead of going straight home, she went to the police station and asked to speak to the inspector leading the investigation, Enzo Carlisi.

"Any news?" asked Flora.

"Nothing yet."

"But it happened two weeks ago. Haven't you handed out the identity profiles I drew for you?"

"Of course we have. Your drawings are perfect, madam, but if those really are the two men who robbed you, they are unknown to the police."

"Really? Are you sure?" Flora was shocked.

"Quite sure. We ran your drawings through the computer and there were no matches. And you yourself said that they were unarmed. If they don't walk around with a gun, it's possible that they didn't intend to kill your fiancé. The results of the autopsy showed that his death was caused by a trauma to the head, which means that they will be charged with aggravated robbery. It's quite possible that they usually just steal bags from old ladies."

"Do you only run your identity profiles through the computer?" said Flora. "I mean, I would have thought the first thing a detective would do is ask his informers if they have seen those men."

"We have asked, madam, but unfortunately without results."

Flora nodded. "Fine," she said, "could I have a photocopy of my drawings, please?"

"Why do you want a copy of your drawings?"

"To save me the trouble of having to draw them again."

"Why ever do you want to draw them again? You're not going to personally look for these men, are you? You should leave the detective work to the professionals."

"You think so? 'Professional' isn't exactly what I'd call the people doing the detective work in this place." Her response annoyed the inspector, who said:

"Unfortunately your drawings are now part of the dossier concerning the investigation, and I have no intention of getting them out for you."

Flora pushed her chair back and stood up.

"Fine. I'll draw them again. And I'll find the people who

killed my fiancé before you do. You are all incompetent!"

She left the room, slamming the door behind her.

"Well," said the inspector to the policewoman who was filing the statements, "I would call that insulting a public official. I'm almost tempted to report her."

The policewoman shook her head. "Let it go," she replied. "She's just pissed off. Do you know what she said to me when she asked to speak to you? That she'd only left hospital an hour ago."

* * *

Flora couldn't put it off any longer; she had to return to the villa. Everything was silent; it was if the birds in the garden were holding their song out of respect for Flavio.

The first thing she did was to put the clothes she'd worn at the hospital into the washing machine. Then she went into the kitchen to see if there was anything still edible that she could have for dinner. She found pasta, biscuits and a carton of milk that was still within its use-by date, but decided it wasn't enough, and so she went out to buy fruit, vegetables, and anything else she might need.

Life had to go on. Those little things, like going out to the supermarket and preparing dinner, would delay the moment when the enormity of the tragedy would finally hit her.

That moment arrived after dinner. Flora didn't feel like watching TV, so she went into the study to open the post that had arrived while she was away, aware that there could be a couple of bills to pay. Among the circulars, she found a couple of letters addressed to Flavio, letters about work he would never read. She felt her heartbeat quicken; she couldn't face opening those letters, but neither could she throw them away. Eventually she decided to put them into the drawer where Flavio kept his tax returns, as no one would ever open that drawer again. But in the drawer, she found something that made her catch her breath.

It was the drawings for the villa that her lover had designed for her. On the plan there were notes, such as 'painting room' and 'Flora's bathroom,' all written in Flavio's elegant handwriting. She looked up, her eyes full of tears, at the walls that screamed 'Flavio's gone forever.'

It was then that she finally felt it, felt the pain of his absence as it tore through her chest and she shouted, screamed like a wounded animal, and threw everything that was on the desk onto the floor. Gasping for breath, she ran out of the room, and went to get her drawing materials.

Paper, pencils, paintbrushes. Her hands shook but Flora forced them to obey her because she had to draw those faces again.

Yes, she had to draw those two terrible faces.

* * *

Flora didn't paint anything else for a long time. She didn't feel like staying at the villa, and anyway there was something else more important she had to do.

She knew full well that she was risking her life by wandering through the most dangerous neighbourhoods of the city, but she was tough by nature, and if anything, the trauma she had suffered had made her even stronger. She felt a ferocity inside her that was ready to explode should any man have tried to molest her, but just to be on the safe side she armed herself with a large knife. With no means to defend herself other than the knife in her pocket, she stopped at the bars frequented by the worst types of men: the drunks, the drug addicts, the tattooed lorry drivers, anyone that is, who had a touch of villainy about them. In her pocket, alongside her knife, she carried money to pay for information and her identity profiles, which she showed to everyone she met, asking the same question each time:

"Do you know these two men?"

Most of the men she showed the picture to said no, but there were some who couldn't resist trying it on with her: 'I'll give you what you want if you give me what I want' they leered. She had done everything she could to appear as ugly and as undesirable as possible to those men: she wore old baggy clothes that hid her slim body, her face was bare and partially covered by a large pair of fake glasses, and her blond hair was scraped back into a bun. But it's an indisputable fact that there are some men who will try it on with anything with a penetrable orifice.

It was dangerous work. One evening a homeless man said: "These two here? I've never seen the fat one, but the thin one... I don't know him but I know where he lives."

Flora's heart lurched. "Could you show me?"

"How much will you give me if I do?"

The man was dressed in rags; he must be in dire need of money.

"Fifty euros?"

"That'll pay for two evenings worth of beer, but I'm pretty sure that this information is worth a lot more to you."

"A hundred euros, and that's my final offer."

The tramp smiled, made a sign for her to follow him, and left the bar. They had been walking for a while when he suddenly stopped.

"Here we are. The guy lives in that building."

He was pointing at a squalid three-storey building, but as Flora stared at it, perplexed, she felt an arm wrap itself around her neck, almost strangling her, and smelt the tramp's rancid breath as he whispered into her ear:

"What do you want from the guy, eh? Is it something I can give you? Mine's bigger, do you want to see it?"

A wave of panic seized her, but then she remembered the knife in her coat pocket: she pulled it out with her free hand and plunged it back as far as she could into the tramp's stomach. The man shouted, loosening his grip on her, and she ran off without looking back.

She had no intention of reporting the incident to the police, and knew full well that the tramp, if he survived the attack, wouldn't report her either. Hang on a second. No, it was too dangerous to let him live. He would tell anyone who would listen that a strange blonde woman was going round showing the identity profiles of the two thugs, and that she was armed. If the police didn't find her, the criminal underworld would.

With her heart in her mouth, Flora retraced her steps. What she was about to do was terrible, but it needed to be done.

The tramp was lying on the ground, moaning; nobody had seen him.

She went up to him holding the knife.

"Why?" he whimpered.

"I'm sorry," replied Flora, and with surgical precision, sliced his carotid artery.

That very same night she buried the knife in her garden.

* * *

The robbery that led to Flavio's death had taken place next to Cinema Lido. Could the two thieves live in the neighbourhood? Were they really that stupid that they robbed people in their own back yard without covering their faces?

But anything is possible, and with this in mind Flora decided to return to the area and ask at the bar next to the cinema. It was vital that she wasn't recognised, and so she disguised herself as an old woman, with a grey wig, old baggy clothes bought at the second hand market, and a gypsy shawl. It was also less probable that someone would try and rape her, which was a relief, as after the episode with the tramp she no longer carried a weapon.

She had read a report of his murder in the papers: following the discovery of the tramp's body, they said, the police were looking for a forty-year old blonde woman who was seen leaving the bar with him…but she wasn't worried; she was only thirty-one years old, and with this new disguise, she looked at least sixty.

"Have you ever seen these people?" she asked the barman at the bar next to the cinema.

"No," he replied, but his eyes told her otherwise. The man was lying.

"Are they in some sort of trouble?" He was the first person who had asked.

"I don't know. My grandson hangs around with them. If they are as bad as they look, I'd rather he found some other friends," she replied.

The barman didn't believe her.

"Out with it lady," he sneered, "you're from the police aren't you."

"You couldn't be more mistaken. But if seeing these faces makes you think of the police, I'm pretty sure you know them."

The barman had been caught out in a lie and didn't know what else to say.

"Now it's your turn to tell the truth," said Flora. "Who are they?"

"I've seen them a couple of times in here, but I don't know who they are."

"Great. So if I were to sit here, at this bar, every evening, there's a chance that in about a week, I'll see them, right?"

"I wouldn't advise it," said the man, shortly.

"Why?"

"If you go looking for trouble, you'll find it."

'He knows them!' she thought to herself.

"The bar is a public place which means that if I pay for what I consume, and don't cause any trouble, I can come here whenever I want," said Flora coldly. "And now I'd like something to drink. I'll have one of those fruit juices with rum, the kind of thing they sell at the disco."

"You don't even know its name," jeered the barman.

"No. I'm too old to go dancing on an evening."

"I don't believe you're that old," said the barman giving her a searching look as he served her drink. "That'll be three euros. And after you've finished, I would be grateful if you left."

Flora drank her drink, paid the barman, and left the bar, but she knew that she was finally on the right track. She returned the following evening.

"The same as I had yesterday, please. Pineapple juice with rum."

The barman gave her a sideways glance, but had no choice but to serve her. She sat down at the table and sipped her drink, lingering over it for as long as she dared. She hoped she would see Flavio's killers come into the bar, but then what? She wouldn't be able to go up to them unarmed. Maybe she should just follow them to see where they lived, all she had to do was follow one…

But nothing happened that evening, nor the following evening. Flora became a regular client; the other customers thought she was an old drunk with no place to go, and they left her alone. She wasn't bothering anyone and even the barman stopped trying to move her on. Evidently he knew that the thugs were of the worst sort, but they weren't his friends. Otherwise he would have warned them and they would have hot-footed it to the bar to see her off.

It was during the tenth evening, while she was sipping her rum, that Flora heard a strange conversation between two men sat at the table behind her.

"Five thousand now and five thousand when the job's done," said Voice Number One. The other person didn't reply, but Flora had the impression that he agreed.

"Don't you want to ask me anything?" asked Voice Number One.

"I never ask questions. The less I know about the victim the better," said Voice Number Two.

"Perfect. I'll read the news in the papers. If everything goes to plan, I'll see you back here on Thursday to give you the other half of the money."

Christ, thought Flora, a contract killing! What else could it be? I hope they don't notice me; they'll probably think I'm drunk, and as they can only see my grey wig, that I'm deaf too.

She wanted to see their faces but she couldn't turn around otherwise they would know that she'd heard them. She pulled a mirror out of her old bag and pretended to be looking at something in her mouth, angling the mirror in such a way that she was able to see the men sat behind her. The man commissioning the killing, who was old and rough looking, was pushing an envelope towards the second man, who was younger and more attractive. Flora memorised their faces.

* * *

On Thursday she was sat in a corner of the bar. She was hoping to see the killer and his boss again, and that they would choose a table as far away from her as possible, as she didn't want to give them the impression that she was interested in them. She didn't need to hear what they were saying. A glimpse of the money would be enough.

There they were. The older man came in first, followed by his henchman five minutes later. Their brief conversation was concluded with an envelope being handed to the younger man, which she understood to mean 'job done', and then the meeting was over.

Flora had read the newspapers to see if there had been any murders reported recently: other than those where the killer had been arrested immediately, there was only one unsolved involving a local businessman who had refused to pay protection money. Poor Corrado Pantani, an innocent father of two children, killed with two shots to the head while he closed his shop for the night...

If he was the subject of the discussion at the bar that evening, then this wasn't a private matter such as that between a husband and wife; this was Mafia business. Flora knew the trouble she was getting into, but by now she didn't care.

She had perfected her disguise using the skills she had learnt in art class, but painted with greasepaint instead of normal paint, and used her face in front of the mirror as a canvas. She knew all about the effects of colour, and light and shade, and when she had finished, her face and hands were speckled with sunspots and she could have easily passed for a seventy year-old. Only a close observer would have noticed that her mouth was young; the thin, dry lips of the old are impossible to recreate with a paintbrush.

With one eye on the men, she finished her rum and yawned loudly, then she blew her nose and inspected the dirty tissue carefully. She was acting the part to perfection, and when she left the bar no one would have guessed that she was following one of the men who had left a moment before.

Flora had chosen the younger one.

She followed him, quickening her step to keep up — the killer was walking too quickly for an authentic old person — until they reached his car, which was parked in the same empty square where Flavio had been killed.

"Excuse me!" shouted Flora.

The young man turned towards her, and seeing the tramp from the bar, said:

"I haven't got any money, lady. Get out of here."

"I don't want your money. I just want a minute of your time."

She held up the identity profiles towards him, which at a distance looked like two carnival masks. Intrigued, he turned away from his car. What harm could a seventy year-old lady armed with two pieces of paper do?

"I want to know if you know them. They've been seen around here," said Flora. If it is a private detective in disguise it's always better to collaborate, thought the young man. He took off his dark glasses, revealing a pair of expressive eyes, artist's eyes, that were incapable of hiding the truth.

"I've never seen them before in my life," said the young man, but his eyes were telling a different story.

"But with a bit of hard work, you could find them for me, couldn't you," insisted Flora, "and bring me their heads on a plate if I paid you enough."

The young man started. How could the woman know who he was, and how dare she talk to him like that. He took out his pistol.

"Get away from me!" he said, "Beat it, otherwise I'll fill you with so many holes, they'll be draining pasta through your body."

"I'm not the police. I want to pay you. These two thugs killed my husband and I want them dead."

By now it was obvious from the woman's voice that she wasn't old and the astonished man panicked. He pointed the pistol towards her.

"Search me," said Flora quickly, "give me a chance, search me!" and she put her hands in the air. The young man stopped for a second, undecided; he was afraid that she wasn't alone, but he decided to follow his instincts. He grabbed Flora's arm and bundled her into his car, muttering: "you wanted to follow me, it's your loss. You're going to have the pleasure of my company for at least another hour because we're going for a long drive, and if I notice that someone is following us, I'll kill you. First you, and then your friends."

"I haven't got any friends," she said sadly. "If I did, I wouldn't have to ask someone like *you* to avenge the death of my husband."

The killer looked at her curiously for a moment, and then started the car. Incredibly, once Flora was certain that the killer was really taking her with him, she relaxed.

* * *

He took her to an abandoned factory that stank of excrement: it was the kind of place where local drug addicts went to shoot up. The killer pushed the woman inside which such force that she fell to the ground.

"What are you waiting for?" said Flora. "Police sirens? They're not coming, my friend."

He didn't reply.

"My name is Flora Persici and I'm a painter."

"Yeah right. And my name's Brad Pitt, and I'm an actor."

"If you weren't so dark, I could well believe you. You're not bad looking," retorted Flora in mocking tone of voice that no old lady would have used. The young man looked at her closely.

"Now that you're actually looking at me, I'm going to perform a bit of magic. Please don't shoot me while I change my appearance."

The first thing she did was take off her grey wig and throw it into the corner.

Away went the glasses and the shawl, then she untied her blond hair and wiped her face clean of make up. The whole operation only took a few seconds. The killer stared at her with his mouth open.

"Flora Persici, painter," she said again, holding out her hand, but the young man refused to take it.

"Jesus Christ," he said, shaking his head.

"I told you so. There's no point looking for a trap that doesn't exist. There's no police, I painted the identity profiles of the two men. I want them dead."

"Why did you come to me?"

Flora sidestepped the question by pulling out a

picture of Flavio.

"My husband," she said, showing it to the killer. "He was killed in the same spot where you parked your car this evening. They killed him because he didn't have enough money."

She always called Flavio 'her husband', not because she was ashamed of cohabiting with him, but because the word 'lover' would have demeaned the bond she had with him. 'Lover' made her think of a squalid tryst between a playboy and a married woman, or between a middle-aged man and a much younger woman. A lover could be a temporary companion, while she had chosen Flavio to be her companion for life. For life. Her eyes filled with tears, and suddenly the killer decided he believed her.

"Fine. You're not from the police. You're a painter and they killed your husband. But what were you doing in that bar, disguised as an old hag? Were you spying on me? Who told you to spy on me?"

"I go every evening to look for my husbands killers. I'm positive they come from that area. It was just a coincidence that I overheard your conversation with your client this evening. I swear it was a coincidence."

"What did you hear?"

"That you are a killer. That you killed someone for ten thousand euros, five thousand as a down payment, and five thousand once the job was done. Do you really believe that I'm going to tell all of this to the police? No, and I'll tell you for why: because I need you to do a job for me."

"You've got a vivid imagination, missy. I carry a weapon because I've got stuff to deal with, but I don't kill for money. If the police don't arrive within the next ten minutes, I'll let you live. But don't ever come looking for me again."

Flora would have welcomed the opportunity to join Flavio in the next world, but being dismissed with a refusal was something she couldn't accept. She played her last card.

"Let's see if I can guess. Corrado Pantani?"

The killer flinched when he heard the name of his most recent victim. He got his pistol out again and pressed its cold barrel against the temple of this woman who continued to provoke him.

"Great," said the woman, "kill me because you haven't got a choice. I know who you are. Either you kill me, or you agree to work for me."

"You're crazy. If you knew why Corrado Pantani was killed, you would know that I don't work for private customers, I work for the Mafia."

"What difference does it make? Is it the cost?"

"I'm not going to kill those two thugs and I don't particularly want to kill you either. Now get out of here before I change my mind."

"I've also got ten thousand euros, and I'll have more once I sell a few paintings. It won't take long."

"It's got nothing to do with money. I can't kill two men without knowing whether my boss wants them alive or dead. I answer to him, not you."

That was the reason behind his refusal and it was a good one; she couldn't argue with it.

Flora felt her world crumble around her; over the last couple of days she had convinced herself that finally she would have the opportunity to avenge Flavio's murder, and now this killer was her only hope.

"You will work for me!" she shouted. "You saw what I'm capable of. I followed a killer! I risked my life! Nothing scares me! Nothing! If one of your Mafia bosses has a problem with the death of those two scum bags, tell him that it was me who killed them. Send him to me!"

The young man shook his head. "You don't give up, do you? I'm off. You can do anything you want. Goodbye."

He started to walk away but Flora threw herself on the ground and grabbed his ankle.

"Wait!" she screamed. "You know them. At least tell me where they live and I'll kill them with my own hands! Tell me where I can find them!"

He tried to free himself from her grip, but tripped and fell to the ground. He felt like hitting her and raised his arm, but stopped when he noticed how beautiful she was. A beautiful woman, desperate but determined, who continued shouting:

"I'll kill those bastards! I can't go on living after they killed my husband! Don't you understand? Do you know what it means to lose the person you loved your whole life? Have you ever loved anyone?"

The young man felt something that he had never felt before: pity. He realised that he would never be able to abandon Flora in this place, sobbing on the floor of a ruined factory and without the means to return home. What should he do? He moved closer to the woman, pushed the hair away from her tearstained face, and looked carefully at her. 'Kill her' said his head, 'she knows everything about you, kill her,' but something else, just as powerful inside him wouldn't let him, leaving him with only one alternative.

"Let's get out of here."

Flora thought she had misheard him. "What?"

"Get up. We'll talk about it somewhere else. The local smack heads could arrive at any moment."

She had won. Smiling, she dried her tears.

"I don't really know everything about you. For starters, I don't even know your name."

"Antonio Santarosa. Tony to my friends."

"Okay Tony. Let's go to my villa. But first you're going to have to take me to the car park next to the bar. I need to pick up my car."

* * *

When they got to the villa, she left Tony in the living room and went to wash her face. He was admiring the paintings, the embroidered curtains, the antique furniture, and everything else that was beautiful about the house when she appeared before him, wearing a slinky dress that made the most of her slender body, and with a touch of make up that was very different to that which she used in her disguise as an old lady. Christ she was beautiful! And going on her house, rich too! I'll never get a woman like that, he thought bitterly. What could a boy from the streets hope for from a woman like her? The only thing he could do was to increase his price. She had a vendetta against those two thugs and she was willing to pay whatever he wanted. She had a beautiful house. It was time for her to show him the money.

"Now," said the young man, "this is the size of it. I work for the Agosta family and those two men work for the Giancola family. I don't know them, I don't even know their names, but I've seen them around and I'm pretty sure that the fat one is a driver for Davide Giancola."

"Are the Giancolas and Agostas allies?"

"No, enemies. Rivals. But I prefer to keep out of all that. From what you've told me these two have made a big mistake. Davide Giancola's driver can't be going around robbing people: his job is to drive and that's all he should be doing. The thinner one has to keep an eye on a certain neighbourhood, tell his boss if he sees a dealer from a rival family on his patch. Giancola has never given them permission to kill people."

"That'll be why the police don't know them," said Flora. "When I showed them the drawings, they just shrugged."

"Exactly," continued Tony, "and if Giancola knew what they were up to, he would be the first person to want them dead. There are rules in the Mafia families that are respected; the most important is that each person does what they're told to do and nothing more. Let's say the driver is caught red handed robbing someone; they would take him to the police station, and then what?"

"They'll find out that he's a driver for Giancola which means that the boss will come under police scrutiny?" hazarded Flora.

"Police scrutiny isn't the half of it. He'd be fucked. The police have been trying to find a reason to arrest Giancola for the past fifteen years. They'll start negotiating with the driver; they'll say things like: 'give us something that could help us incriminate your boss and we'll let you go'."

"Which is why Giancola would rather they were dead than arrested."

"Exactly. Maybe if I were to kill them I would be doing Giancola a favour, but it wouldn't go down too well with my boss. He would rather the driver continued robbing people, is arrested, talks too much, and takes Giancola down with him. If the Giancolas were to disappear, the Agostas would have a more of the city under their control. Anyway, there's no point speculating; I might work for the

Agostas, but because I'm not a member of the 'family' I'm neutral. If there is someone who is bothering the Agostas, they get me to kill him, leaving them free to get their alibis sorted: papa Agosta, his brother, his son, his uncle, his brother-in-law or whoever, all have an alibi for the time the crime was committed. Which is why the police never have enough evidence to arrest them."

Flora sighed. "Are you going to do the job for me or not? Yes or no?"

"It's not that easy. First of all, I've got to be sure that no one will know that it was me. Not even my boss must know. Then I don't know what risks I'll be taking. Killing two thugs isn't as easy as killing a poor defenceless wretch who doesn't want to pay protection money. Let's say I shoot the driver and he shoots back? Then what?"

"I get it. I have to pay you compensation for the risks you'll be taking," said Flora.

"Twenty thousand for each man."

"I haven't got forty thousand, but I'll sell my cottage in the country if you swear to me that you won't change your mind. I'm fond of that cottage."

Tony smiled. "It's been a pleasure doing business with you madam."

* * *

Over the next couple of days, Flora learnt from Tony that the names of the driver and his accomplice were respectively Carlo Mazzola and Saverio Tulli. An action plan was devised, and on the third Tuesday in April the painter was sat alone in her villa waiting to receive a telephone call and the anonymous message 'mission accomplished'.

But it wasn't the telephone that rang: at ten o'clock that evening, someone rang the doorbell. Despite the late hour, she went to open the door, knowing it could only be Tony. He was standing on the front step, nervous, sweating, his right hand holding his left shoulder.

"Oh my God!" she exclaimed. "Are you hurt?"

"Yes. It's nothing serious. But not everything went according to plan."

Flora closed the door behind him.

"Shall I call a doctor?"

"No. The bullet isn't inside the wound. It just glanced my shoulder. Even if it were inside, the last thing we need is a doctor asking awkward questions. Do you know how to treat a wound?"

"I'll give it a go," she said, looking worriedly at the blood.

"I know what you're thinking. Those two are dead. Your man's murder has been avenged. Happy now?"

"So what went wrong then?"

"I'll tell you after you've patched up my shoulder. Christ Almighty! I didn't know where else to go. I've never been shot before."

"It doesn't matter. You can stay here for as long as you like."

"I might well have to. If you've got me into trouble, it'll be up to you to hide me."

Flora decided not to ask him anything else as she had noticed the tension in the young man's voice. She led him into the bathroom, sat him down on a stool, and started to take off his blood soaked jacket and shirt. His chest was slim but muscular and she stared at it for a second while she assessed his wound. She then went over to the medical cabinet and took a couple of things out. She started dabbing iodine over the wound, and Tony, feeling it sting, stifled a cry.

"It won't be difficult to find clothes that fit you," said Flora after she had disinfected the wound. "You're the same size as Flavio."

"Really? Why have you still got his clothes? He's been dead a month, hasn't he?"

"I haven't had time to sort things out," she replied, cutting a strip of gauze. "Immediately after the attack, I was hospitalised with shock and then, as soon as I was discharged, I started looking for the killers. In other words, I haven't spent much time in the villa. I've also been neglecting my painting, which is a problem as I've got an exhibition next month to prepare for."

She applied the gauze and a plaster and then said: "All done. I'll just get you a shirt and a jacket.

"Wait!" shouted Tony. He tried to lift his left arm but after a couple of centimetres he stopped and let out a groan.

"Just as I feared. I won't be able to get my arm into the shirt sleeve, the wound is too painful."

"What shall we do?" She thought for a moment, and then said:

"I'll give you my poncho. You won't have to move your shoulder."

"No way! That thing is for women."

"And who's going to be looking at you? I'd be the only one laughing at you, if that's what you want."

Flora went to get the poncho, and although he didn't much like the idea, he sighed with relief when he felt its warmth.

"As if I haven't suffered enough," he muttered. "Thanks."

"Now will you tell me what happened?"

Tony sighed. "I didn't have many problems with the

driver. At seven o'clock he went to park his boss's car in the garage then turned towards home. I waited until he was at the entrance. He was alone and I was positioned a couple of metres away: I shot him in the head.

However, someone in his house heard the shot and I saw a window being opened. It's possible that someone in his family saw me from behind the shutters but I had a stocking over my face so they would only be able to describe my build. I'm more worried about what happened next —" He stopped.

"Carry on, I'm listening," said Flora.

"Saverio Tulli was stationed in his normal spot which, at half past eight in the evening, is in Piazza Sette Cavalli. At that time, the square's full of dealers and kids looking for drugs, and Saverio was there to keep an eye on things. This evening though, he wasn't alone. He spent the whole time I was there talking to a sixteen or seventeen year-old who I'd never seen before. I don't know whether the kid was new to the area and wanted to know where to find some blow, and Saverio was making him work for the information, because it's not as if you can say to the first person who passes: 'I know everything there is to know about the drugs scene,' but the fact remains that the young man didn't go away. So I thought: I'll shoot now, and I won't bother killing the lad too, because I've got a stocking over my face so he'll never be able to identify me. I got out of my car and got as close as I needed to shoot Saverio in the head. I thought that the lad would have taken to his heels, but do you know what he did? He pulled out a pistol and shot me."

"Christ!" exclaimed Flora. "So that's why he managed to hit you. He caught you by surprise!"

"Yes. And he hadn't finished; he wanted to kill me, so

I had to kill him."

"Does that mean I'll have to pay you for three murders?"

"It's not funny, Flora. I don't know who that lad was. It's the first time that I've killed someone without knowing who they are."

"What difference does it make? He was an armed scum bag like all the rest."

"It's not my conscience that's bothering me," replied Tony. "It's the possible retribution from the relatives of the scum bag."

"I see," said Flora, "Tomorrow I'll buy the papers; they'll give us the guy's name. In the meantime, you should rest. Do you want something to eat?"

Tony shook his head. "I need to use the bathroom and then I'll go to bed. Better still, a painkiller would be good."

"Alright. I'll make up the bed in the guest bedroom. The poncho won't be that comfortable to sleep in, but it's better than nothing. I've got some ibuprofen. You're not allergic, are you?"

"No," he replied, "At least I hope not."

* * *

The next morning Tony woke up hungry. Flora had laid the table with a generous breakfast — milk, coffee, three types of biscuits, jam — and had gone out early to get the papers.

When she returned, they both studied the day's news carefully.

"Listen to this," said Flora. "Three dead in two different shootings. One killer?"

"That's the one. What does it say?"

"Carlo Mazzola, driver, was killed in an ambush outside

his house with a shot to the head. Less than two hours later, two young men known to Mazzola, were killed in the same way, and the police believe that the murders are connected. The other two victims are: Saverio Tulli, twenty four, and Giuseppe Giancola, seventeen. None of the victims were known to the police."

Tony went white. "Did you say Giuseppe Giancola? Oh God!"

"Is he the son of the boss?"

"No, otherwise I would have recognised him. He was his brother's son. Shit! I've killed someone from the family."

"But if no one saw you, why is it a problem? Look, here it says that Mazzola's wife saw a black man running away. That's funny! Were you dressed as a African?"

"No."

"Then why did that idiot say —" she stopped herself. It was obvious.

"A red herring," murmured Tony, "to throw the police off the scent. That's what the Mafia families always do; they'll want to take care of things themselves. Signora Mazzola saw her husband being shot and told his boss. When he heard about the other two murders a couple of hours later, Giancola would have called the widow back saying: 'get the cops looking for a black man.'"

Flora nodded. "So while the police are off chasing a phantom black man, the Giancolas have time to look for the killer. What's the likelihood that they'll find out that it was you?"

"I don't know. Some of the kids in the square where I killed the boys could have seen my car. Giancola will have them all questioned."

"Do you really think that a kid off his head on cocaine

would have enough wits about him to take down the plate number of a car belonging to someone he doesn't give a shit about?"

"Quite possibly, in the hope that it'll earn him a couple of free grams."

Flora thought for a moment. "Let's say that they find out who the car is registered to. How would they find out that you are here?"

"And how long do you think I can stay here? Ten years?"

He started to list the problems with his current situation, but Flora was determined to find a solution.

"What would happen," she asked, "if you were to ask the Agostas for help?"

"There are two possibilities. The first is that Agosta would hide me, but I'd have to spend the rest of my life working for him for nothing. Basically, I'd become his slave. The second is that he would be angry because I've taken out a Giancola without his permission. He could well deliver me to the enemy as proof that it wasn't him who ordered the murders. No babe, I'm not going to my boss for help. I'm in the shit, and it's all your fault."

"Don't blame me," said Flora. "You could have hired a car and no one would have been any the wiser."

"Yeah right. If they question someone from the car hire firm, they'll talk. And to hire a car you need to show your driving licence and the firm keeps a copy. In other words, it's worse than using your own car. It's the first port of call for the police if they are on the hunt for someone. What makes you think that the Mafia don't know any of this?"

Flora sighed deeply. "Tony, how many people had you killed before we met?"

"Eleven. Fourteen now."

"And you've never been caught."

"Correct."

"If you've got away with it for so long, what makes you think that they'll get you this time?"

"Because this time I've killed the nephew of the boss. They'll turn the world upside down to find me."

"And if I were to help you to escape abroad?"

"That's a great idea. And how am I supposed to live once I get there?"

"When you asked me for forty thousand euros, I put my cottage up for sale to pay you, but it's worth a lot more; I should get at least two hundred thousand for it. If you give me a couple of weeks to find a buyer, and also because we need to wait for your shoulder to heal, I'll be able to give you the two hundred thousand euros and then you can go wherever you want."

Tony's mouth was open with shock.

"Are you sure? You'll put me up for two weeks and then you'll give me all that money?"

"I was the one who got you into this mess, and I'll be the one to get you out of it," she replied. "No one will come looking for you here, but if your car is nearby, you'd best get rid of it immediately."

"You're right. It's parked right outside," said Tony.

"Give me the keys."

"My poor car. What are you going to do with it?"

"I'll leave it at the airport and I'll take a taxi home. No one should find it there, but if they do, they'll think you've flown abroad."

He stared at her with growing admiration. He had never met a woman who was so quick to make rational decisions in times of stress.

"You're a criminal mastermind!" he exclaimed. "You

sound like the kingpin of operations!"

"I'm only a painter," she said sadly, "but something changed the day my love was killed in such a barbaric way. I don't think there's anything I'm not capable of doing anymore. I've even stabbed a tramp."

"Really? Why?"

"I was looking for information about the murderers, and the tramp had me believe that he knew something. He took me to a deserted street and tried to rape me, but I had a knife."

Tony smiled. "Did you stick it into his balls?"

"No my friend. I cut his throat. He's dead."

Tony was struggling to take it all in. "Bloody hell! Where's the knife now?"

"Buried in my garden. I'm the only one who goes in there so no one will ever find it."

"Then you really are capable of anything."

"Yes. And as you've avenged the death of Flavio, I promise I'll save you. Let's not waste any more time. Give me the keys to your car."

He tossed them to her and she was out the door before he had time to say goodbye.

* * *

Once she had hidden Tony's car, all that remained for them to do was to wait for the two hundred thousand euros needed for his escape. In the meantime, Flora started painting again as there was only a few days left before the inauguration of her show; she had promised the organisers twenty paintings and the twentieth was still unfinished.

Tony's convalescence was unhindered by fever or

infection, so he wandered freely around the villa, and was enchanted when he found the painter absorbed in her latest work. It showed a sunset over the sea, and the light reflected in the water was a captivating spectrum of colour, but the beach itself was squalid and dirty. A dead seagull with rigid claws and with his swollen chest turned to the sky, lay on the sand next to sacks of rubbish, broken bottles, and beer cans.

"Holy Christ!" said Tony over Flora's shoulder, making her jump.

'Oh Flavio, Flavio. I thought it was you!'

She stopped for a moment as she struggled to fight the sadness that washed over her, and then, when she had composed herself, turned to face Tony.

"Do you like it?"

"Of course I do. It's a bit different. Why did you put all that rubbish under such a beautiful sunset?"

"It's up to the viewer to put their own interpretation on it. What's yours?"

"I'm no art critic."

"I'd much rather have the opinion of a normal person."

Tony thought for a moment. "Well, we could say that nature's dying and that we are heading towards the end of the world. It was man who poisoned the seagull and polluted the beach. It's like reprimand to man."

"Perfect," said Flora. "Now what if I'd painted the sun at midday and children playing on the beach among the rubbish, wouldn't that be a reprimand to man too?"

Tony sighed. "I don't know why, but I don't like the second version as much. A sunset is a more powerful expression; it's the day that's dying, it's death. There shouldn't be any children on the beach because they symbolise new life. The beach should be deserted like it is in the picture."

Flora turned, shocked to find such sensitivity in a man who killed for money. She had just heard the kind of shrewd comment that was Flavio's speciality and, God. She had just heard a ghost.

"What's the matter?" asked Tony when he saw her white face.

"Nothing," she replied with a sad smile. "Welcome to the world of art, Tony."

She was so close to him that he was overwhelmed by the urge to kiss her, but at that moment his telephone rang and the magic was gone.

"Hello? Yes? Uncle wants to see me?" He was speaking in code; uncle must be the boss of the Agosta family.

"No, tell him I can't. No, I can't do any jobs for him for the time being. Why? Because I'm not well. I've got leukaemia and I'm in hospital for chemotherapy. Oh for Christ's sake, I'm not going to tell you which hospital. It's none of your business. I'm ill and I don't want to do a job for him. I think I might be dying, okay? Say hi to Uncle." Furious, he turned off his phone.

"What's going on," asked Flora.

"It's all over. I can never work for the Agostas again. I don't what I'm going to do now."

"Have you forgotten about the two hundred thousand euros? What about opening a shop selling Italian shoes abroad? Foreigners would pay a pretty price for Italian leather."

"You mean I should go into trade? I don't really think that's my thing."

"What you really mean that you can't see yourself doing an honest job."

"Get on with your painting."

Flora picked up her paintbrush and murmured:

"I've never asked you why you became a killer. Will you tell me?"

He was silent for a while and she was afraid that she had offended him, but after a couple of minutes he started to speak.

"You wouldn't believe it, but I come from a pretty good home. My father was a policeman."

"Interesting. Continue."

"A violent policeman who beat up the criminals he caught, and he was forever being cautioned by his bosses for violating their rights. His reputation meant he was never promoted and he took out his frustrations at work on his family. He would come home angry and hit my mother. Sometimes he would hit me too, but most of all he would hit my mother, and I hated him because my mother was an angel. As a child, I swore that I would get my own back by becoming a gangster. The opposite of Papà. You know how children's minds work, or maybe you don't; it doesn't matter. By the time I was fourteen, I was taking my father's pistol while he slept to practice my shot in the courtyard. When he noticed I said: 'Papà, I want to become a policeman like you.' He believed me; he didn't seem particularly worried about the risks of a young guy wandering around with a loaded gun. I don't think he loved me, and I doubt he realised I hated him. My dream was to wait until he was an old man, and then one day say to his face: 'look at me, you bastard, I'm a gangster!' I wanted him to become so old and weak that he would be powerless to react, I wanted to watch his face crumple with pain and anger when I said: 'I work for the Mafia!' Imagine if he had had a heart attack on hearing the news? I would have been so happy!" Then

Tony stopped. Evidently things hadn't gone to plan.

"What happened?"

"He'll never grow old, that's what happened. He was killed during a robbery when he was only fifty years old and I was twenty. My life as a gangster had just started, all I'd had to do was make friends with an old school friend whose parents were in the Mafia, but my father didn't know anything about my chosen profession. He died a hero, and my mother was left a widow with her husband's pension. Nobody hit her anymore. You would think it was a happy ending, but it wasn't. In my mother's eyes, my father was a hero, even though he had hit her regularly throughout their marriage. He was a hero who died doing his duty as a policeman, and she boasted about him. Her pride was the only thing she had left. Three cheers for the police! How could I tell her what I'd become? It would have been a terrible blow to her; she would have been so disappointed in me. The pain I'd wanted to inflict on Papà would be hers. I no longer dared look her in the eyes, and shortly afterwards I left home and I've never been back."

"That's awful!" said Flora. "Have you got any brothers or sisters?"

"I had a sister who died of meningitis when she was six years old."

"So you're an only child who's abandoned his mother. Don't you realise how much she must be suffering, the poor woman?"

"She would suffer a lot more if she knew what I did for a living."

"You could have invented something! You could have said you were a truck driver or something."

"I can't lie," said Tony. Shocked, Flora stopped painting and turned round.

"Is that a joke?"

"No. I can lie to someone on the telephone but not face to face. My eyes betray me every time."

She put down her paintbrush. "It's true," she murmured. "I remember the day we met. I showed you the drawings of those men and you said you didn't know them, but I didn't believe you for one second."

Tony didn't say anything. She went up to him and looked closely into his sad eyes.

"Your eyes are telling me that you miss your mother."

"Of course I miss her, but there's nothing I can do about it."

"Do you have anyone in your life? A girlfriend, for example?"

"I make a living killing people. What kind of girl wants a killer? A prostitute who would sell me down the river for a hundred euros?"

"You were a killer, Tony. Past tense. Don't you realise everything's changed? You're going to go abroad and you're going to find yourself a normal job. Promise me that once you're settled, you'll write to your mother? Nobody will be checking her post seeing that you abandoned her years ago."

The lump in Tony's throat made it difficult for him to speak, so he just nodded. He wanted to shout: there are people who get everything wrong, who make all the wrong decisions, and I'm one of them. I'm under no allusion that I'll change, and I doubt I'll ever find the right girl for me.

'You shouldn't be scared Flora', he thought. 'You shouldn't be scared of loving a killer.' But he didn't dare say anything because he was frightened of how superior she was to him: she was more educated, more refined, more intelligent, maybe even braver. She was forbidden fruit, and aroused in him the same sadness that filled his eyes with tears when he thought of his mother.

Mama. Gone. Lost forever.

* * *

A week later, Flora told Tony that she had found a buyer for the cottage.

"That was quick."

"I know. I asked two hundred and twenty thousand euros. and after a bit of negotiating, I accepted two hundred.That's what I promised you and anyway I won't be left without a cent. My show opens tomorrow, and I'm hoping to earn about ten thousand from the sale of my paintings."

"I'd really like to see them all," said the young man.

"Are you serious? We haven't got much time; two men are coming this evening in a van to take them to the exhibition venue."

"Well you'd better show them to me immediately then. Come on, we've got no time to lose."

Flora led him into the small room where the other paintings had been left to dry.Tony was captivated.

"Which one do you like the most?" she asked.

"The Footpath.That old woman... She looks like she's walking towards her death."

The painter felt her chest tighten as she remembered an almost identical discussion with her dead love.

"It's easy to find a meaning in that painting. Now let's hear what you have to say about this one!" she replied, pointing at another canvas. It showed a young woman in a wedding dress walking down a dingy street lined with crumbling houses, apparently unaware that her veil was being dragged through the mud. There was a bloody paw print on her veil left by a black cat that had just killed a mouse. Impressed, Tony said:

"I don't know. I think you enjoyed creating contrasts between the colours. The white of the bride's dress against the grey of her surroundings, the black cat on the white veil, red blood on white. It's a game of contrasts."

"Anything else?"

"Maybe I've understood. Life is full of these contrasts. The girl is happy because she is about to get married, and so she doesn't see the squalor that surrounds her. All the horrible things are behind her but she's looking ahead. She's walking away from them; she doesn't want to see them."

The painter's throat was tight with emotion.

"My God," she murmured. "Why on earth would a person like you become a hired killer?"

He understood her question but he didn't have an answer ready for her. He said nothing.

"Tony, would you like to learn how to paint?"

"No, because I don't know how to draw. I love art, but there's no point learning how to paint if you don't know how to draw."

"Why don't we have a bit of fun? I'll draw the outlines and you can colour them in."

Tony smiled. "I'm not twelve anymore."

"If it makes you happy, who cares how old you are. If you did know how draw, what would your subject be?"

"I've got something in mind. A cloudy and stormy sky. Rain is falling into a creak at the bottom of a canyon and the banks of the creak are steep and threatening. A lone wolf sits on the edge of the canyon with his face turned up to the sky, howling at the storm.

"Oh!" exclaimed Flora. "I like it, and it should be easy because there aren't any human figures. Human figures are the most difficult things to draw. Shall we paint it together?"

Tony shrugged. He didn't know what else to do.

"What made you think of that scene?" she asked.

"I don't know. Maybe it's because I'm the lone wolf. I want to fight the storm, but its useless trying. The painting represents the futility of the fight against destiny."

"It could also symbolise a nature that is wild and powerful!" observed Flora. "I think it's a great idea. Let's do it."

Tony let himself be led into the painting room. The woman put a clean canvas over the easel, dipped her paintbrush into a mix of colours to create the right shade of grey, and painted the base of the painting. A few strokes marked out the position of the creak and the canyon but the contours of the wolf were clearly defined.

"That's lovely," said Tony, as happy as a child at Christmas. "It's exactly what I had in mind, with the wolf on the right. You read my mind."

"As you don't want to change anything, you can start colouring. Start with the wolf. What colour were you thinking of?"

"Dark brown."

"Grey would be better to create a contrast between light and dark, and to bring out the wolf's coat. You won't get that effect with brown."

"But the sky's stormy," objected Tony. "If I colour the sky grey, the wolf won't stand out from the background."

"It's the same for everything in life: ask yourself a question and try and find the solution," replied Flora lightly. "Start wherever you see fit. The ideas will come as you paint. Here are the smaller paint brushes..."

She was interrupted by a knock at the door. They looked at each other, startled.

"Whoever it is," said Flora, "you're one of my pupils. Now paint!"

She left him there and went to open the door. It was Inspector Carlisi, whom Flora had so considerately called 'incompetent' the last time they had met, accompanied by a young policewoman.

"Oh!" exclaimed the painter, "to what do I owe the honour?"

"It's a courtesy visit. May we come in?"

She waved them to the sofa in the sitting room and the two officers sat down.

"Signora Persici, do you remember the identity profiles you drew for us?"

"Of course I do."

"They have been most helpful. Two men were killed last week whose faces matched the ones you drew exactly."

She pretended to be shocked. "Are you telling me that my husband's killers are dead?"

"That's what it looks like."

"Good. If I were to tell you that I was upset, I would be lying to you."

"Of course. And now you're going to tell us that you know nothing about what happened, aren't you?"

"Inspector, what am I supposed to know?"

"A black man was seen running away from the scene of the first crime. There are no black men working at the villa are there, madam?"

"My cleaner is Sicilian. Feel free to check. She comes on Mondays."

"And the gardener?"

"I look after the garden. Do you think I paid a black man to kill them?"

"We aren't here to accuse you of anything. However, it's quite obvious from your standard of living that you would have the money to pay a black man to kill someone."

"Well, you'll have to proof that I know at least one black man. You may well think me racist but I've never had a black friend, ever."

Tony, who was listening from the painting room, smiled.

"And another thing," continued Flora, "how could I have found the two men on my own?"

"You swore to us that you would find them."

She shrugged. "Easy to say, but a lot harder to do."

"And while we're on the subject," continued the inspector, "despite being very comfortably off, you have put your cottage in the country up for sale. As if you had to give a large sum of money to someone."

"The cottage? I sold it because Flavio is dead. I won't be going there again on my own. It's too sad."

"You could have rented it out," insisted Carlisi. "Why would you sell property now, just as prices are starting to rise, knowing that next year you would have earned at least thirty per cent more? Only someone who needed the money urgently would sell now."

"You're forgetting that I'm an artist not a business woman. It never crossed my mind to wait."

It was about time, Tony decided, to give her a hand. He came into the sitting room and said:

"You're right, my dear. Dark brown for the wolf doesn't work. It looks terrible."

She looked at him astounded. The young man's shirt

was covered in brown brush strokes.

"Do you think I should add a bit of grey?" he continued.

Suddenly she understood. "Yes, add a bit of grey. Be careful. You've got paint everywhere."

"It doesn't matter. Isn't tomorrow laundry day?"

"Get back in there. Can't you see I've got visitors?"

The young man winked at the young policewoman.

"Okay."

"I'm sorry about that," said Flora when he had left. "That's one of my pupils; he can be a little intrusive."

Carlisi and the policewoman exchanged looks.

"No problem. You should get back to your lesson. We won't keep you any longer."

Once they were back in their car, the policewoman said:

"Inspector, I think we're barking up the wrong tree. The young lady's moved on. Did you see what a good looking guy he was?"

"I agree. Who were they trying to kid, calling him her pupil! They live together, he even knows that tomorrow's washing day."

"Exactly," said the policewoman. "And if they're already living together, I doubt the lady's going to waste much time and money going after the killers of an ex-boyfriend. I don't know how some people can move on so quickly. And they seemed so happy! Disgusting."

"It's none of our business," said the inspector, starting the car. "We've got concentrate on finding other people who would have had a grudge against those murdered bastards. It shouldn't be difficult; after all they did go around robbing people."

Inside the villa, Flora and Tony laughed until tears rolled down their cheeks.

* * *

Flora's exhibition was inaugurated on the first of May and would be open until the twenty-fifth. Sicily's mild climate meant that the city was already full of tourists, one of whom, an art-loving German called Gunther Schmidt, paid a visit to Flora's exhibition and fell head over heels for two of the paintings. Herr Schmidt then went to find the gallery director with twelve hundred euros in cash in his pocket, six hundred for each of the paintings.

"I want them now," he said.

"Of course, sir," said the director, "but we'll only be able to give them to you once the exhibition has finished."

"Why?"

"Because we've only been open a day and the paintings are to be exhibited until the twenty-fifth. People have to see them to become familiar with the painter's work. Someone may commission a similar painting to that chosen by you after seeing the 'sold' signing hanging next to it."

The German, who was fifty, balding, and paunchy, spoke a little Italian and probably understood the director's point, although he pretended not to.

"My plane leaves tomorrow," he said. "I no wait for paintings."

"Rest assured sir, we can send the paintings to Germany after the twenty-fifth. All we ask for is a little something to go towards postage and packing..."

"My plane leaves tomorrow with me and with the paintings," insisted the German. His words caught Flora's attention.

"Is there a problem?" she asked.

"The gentleman here," explained the director, "is going back to Germany tomorrow and wants to take the paintings back with him. I'm finding it rather difficult to convince him otherwise."

Flora nodded to the customer and gave his arm a reassuring squeeze.

"I'm the painter," she said.

"Oh! Very, very pleased to meet you," said the German, his face lighting up with pleasure.

"Seeing that you're such a nice man, could I ask you to do me a favour? Would you mind most awfully letting me keep the paintings until the twenty-fifth of May? Once the exhibition is over, a courier will bring them to your house at no extra cost."

"What is courier?"

"A member of my family will personally deliver them to you. It won't cost you anything."

"What if courier damage painting?"

"They won't. And anyway, you don't have to pay for the canvases now. You can give the twelve hundred euros to the courier once you are sure that the paintings are in perfect condition."

Schmidt mulled this over. "I pay in Germany. When delivered?"

"Exactly," said the painter.

"Flora, we can't do that," objected the director.

"Let me handle this for once," she replied. "Please? I have my reasons."

"Fine. Do it your way," said the director as he walked away.

"Okay," said Flora, turning back towards the German, "do we have an agreement? One thousand two hundred euros, to be paid on delivery, and only if the canvases are in perfect condition."

"Yah," said the German, giving Flora his business card with an address in Lipsia and a telephone number, " and here my home."

"Delivery on May twenty-seventh," said Flora. "Okay?"

"Yah, ya. You beautiful woman," added Schmidt, for no particular reason.

She smiled. An idea was forming in her head and as soon as she got home she told Tony.

"You're going to be the delivery boy."

"Why?"

"Because it'll give you an excuse to go to Germany without arousing suspicion. It won't be long before I'll have the two hundred thousand euros; you'll put them in a bag and you'll take the money with you to Germany with the paintings. If anyone asks you what you're doing in Germany, you can say that you're delivering the paintings to Gunther Schmidt, and should the police question your story, tell them to call the German. And that's all there is to it. To make the story even more believable, you'll buy a return ticket, but obviously you'll never use it."

Tony nodded. "It could work," he said, "but I'll have to change my identity. I told the Agostas that I was lying in hospital half dead! What happens if my name appears on the passenger list?"

"Isn't there anyone of your shady acquaintances who could forge you some fake documents?"

"Yes, there is someone. Once, when I needed some documents forged, Agosta sent me to Uncle Cesare. Officially he has an antiques shop — he sells odds and ends that no one in their right mind would ever buy — but at the back he's got all the printing equipment necessary."

"Fantastic," said Flora. "I'll bleach your hair blonde and

then you can go pay Uncle Cesare a visit."

"Hang on a second. This man does favours for the Mafia. He doesn't care which family they come from, as long as they pay him. What if someone from the Giancola family is watching the shop?"

Flora thought for a minute. "I'll go then," she decided.

"It's risky," muttered Tony.

"We haven't got a choice. Here's the plan. Step one: I'll bleach your hair blonde. Since I'm already blonde, the shop assistant will just think that I want to cover my grey hairs. Step two: you'll put on a pair of false reading glasses that will make you look like a high school teacher. Once disguised, you'll get your photo taken in the photo booth at the station, and I'll also tell when we'll go: not in the middle of the day because I don't want my neighbours talking, and not at night otherwise we'll get stopped by the police. No, we'll go at seven in the morning, when the only people who are out and about are those who leave early for work, and they won't give us a second glance. Step three: I'll take the photos to Uncle Cesare and I'll ask him to make a false identity card for a certain. Giovanni Pisano, how does that sound?"

"Well…"

"How old are you Tony?"

"Thirty two."

"Were you born in seventy five? I'll get him to write 1972 because the glasses will make you look older. How much does Uncle Cesare ask?"

"I think...About five hundred euros."

"I can afford that. Where is this antiques shop?"

"Are you sure you want to go, Flora? It's dangerous."

"I told you we don't have a choice. What's the address?"

"Corso Vittorio Emanuele, 134."

"But that's right in the town centre! Uncle Cesare certainly doesn't try to keep a low profile!"

"If you're pretending to run an antiques shop, it makes sense to choose a place which is full of tourists. Every now and then he hoodwinks a poor American into buying a seventies candlestick by telling him that its from the nineteenth century."

Flora smiled. "He sounds like a character. I can't wait to meet him."

* * *

In the antiques shop, Flora loitered over a threadbare silk lampshade that quite probably belonged to the shop owner's aunt and waited for Uncle Cesare, a gaunt seventy year old, to approach her.

"Do you like it madam?"

"Depends on the price," she replied.

"Two hundred euros."

"I'll have to think about it."

The old man came closer and whispered:

"How much were you looking to spend?"

"A lot more. But I'm after something else antique. An identity card."

The man stiffened. "What makes you think I sell antique documents?" he asked, pretending not to understand. "Nobody's interested in them anymore."

"no, but I am. Signor Agosta sent me."

At the mention of his boss, Cesare's behaviour changed. He made an almost imperceptible sign for her to follow him and went into the back of the shop. He closed the curtain to stop any other customers from spying on them — always supposing that customers were to enter that dive — and said, without preamble: "Five hundred euros."

"Two hundred up-front, and three hundred on delivery," Flora shot back.

"Agreed. Have you got the photos, honey?"

Flora got the photos out of her bag and gave them to him. "That's not you," he said, disappointed.

"No, the identity card's not for me, it's for my boyfriend."

"I know that face. Are the police looking for him?"

"No. Write that his name is Giovanni Pisano... Write this down, I don't trust your memory."

The old man went over to an old grimy desk, and picked up a pen and a notepad. "Continue."

"Giovanni Pisano, born on the twenty-seventh of April 1972 in Catania, resident in Palermo at via Tramontana number twenty-six. Single."

"Who is he really?" asked Cesare.

"Giovanni Pratolini, my lover. He wants to leave his wife and run away with me."

"A man of good taste," said the old man, staring at her, but Flora, never once losing her composure, pulled two hundred euros out of her bag.

"What time can I come back tomorrow?"

"Tomorrow's too soon."

"Not if I'm here at seven tomorrow evening. You'll have all the time you need to complete the job."

"Fine, come back at seven. And bring the other three hundred euros with you."

He waited until she had left the shop, before picking up his mobile phone and dialling a number.

"Hello? Signor G? You told me to let you know if a young man came to me for a false document. What does this young man look like? I wouldn't call a shadow that someone saw running off in the dark a detailed description would you? And anyway, I imagine that the young man will try to change his appearance so he'll have a completely different face by now. I know, I know, we can't be sure, but you did say that you trusted my instincts…which is why I'm calling you. I've been asked for a false identity card for a young man who didn't even have the guts to come himself. He sent his woman. The lady will be here tomorrow at seven to collect the documents and you could have her followed to see where she lives and with whom. Don't you think that's a good idea? Obviously I'll need a little something for my trouble. Okay."

He put the phone down with such a large smile that his gaunt face struggled to contain it. The voice on the other end of the phone had said 'a thousand euros now, and another five thousand if it's the man we're looking for.'

* * *

Flora was pretty tired when she returned to the villa as she'd also been to the travel agents to book a plane ticket for the fugitive.

"Tony?" she called, as she came through the door, "Where are you?"

He came out of the painting room. He was blonde, but every attempt to straighten his hair had been useless; it was as soft and wavy as before. He was so good looking.

"All done," she said. "I've got the money, the flight is booked, and by this time tomorrow you'll have your new documents."

"You're fantastic," replied the young man, but there was no pleasure in his eyes. He was staring at her as if he were looking at a photo of a dead relative.

"What were you doing in the painting room?"

"I was finishing the painting of the wolf."

"Really? Let me see it."

Her excitement at seeing a painting that wasn't hers grabbed her by the throat. Technically, Tony had a lot to learn, but the colours he had chosen evoked a landscape that was gloomy and hostile to man. A dark grey with dark purple highlights for the sky, a blackish green for the creak and as for the wolf, dark brown painted over the grey had given it a realistic mottled coat. A wolf that was losing his fur, old and desperate.

"It's nothing special," said Tony, "but I would like you to have it to remind you of me."

"I like it a lot," replied Flora, "but as it's your first work of art, wouldn't you rather take it with you?"

"No. This is my first painting, and it'll be my last because I won't have anyone to teach me how to draw the outlines of the figures."

The woman nodded. "I'll keep it then. Every now and then, I'll look at that lone wolf and think of you."

He was the lone wolf, he was the one who wanted to howl at the sky. Flora sensed his sadness. She turned to look at him, but instead of meeting his eyes, she met his lips.

A second later they were up against a wall, clinging to each other, tearing each other's clothes off, powerless to contain the fury of their passion. Tony winced.

"What's the matter?"

"My bad shoulder... But it's nothing, don't stop. Don't stop!"

He had never desired a woman so much before; the other women had been easy, one night stands, or one week at the most. His life as a professional killer wasn't compatible with emotional ties, and all that love that had been shut away inside him, came pouring out over the woman who had changed his life, she was beautiful, sweet, strong, intelligent; an extraordinary woman who was merciless in her pursuit of revenge yet loyal and honest at the same time. Tony was trying to meld their bodies together, pushing his tongue into her mouth, biting her breasts, his hands slipping further and further down towards the soft mound that was the source of life. She surrendered herself to him, overcome by lust and maybe loneliness too, but her thoughts belonged to another man, the heat she felt belonged to another man, the hands….how far would those hands dare to go?

"Flavio!" she shouted just before she reached the peak of her desire, "Flavio, no!"

Tony pulled away from her suddenly, gasping for breath. It was as if he had suddenly realised that instead of a flower he was cradling a jellyfish that was stinging him.

"What did you say?" he murmured.

"Oh God, I can't. Please forgive me. Forgive me!"

Tony gave her an icy stare and then, to show that there was nothing more to say, he put his shirt and trousers back on.

"Tony, I'm so sorry. It's just too soon. Flavio only died a month and a half ago."

"That's it, is it? So it's got nothing to do with the fact that he was a brilliant architect, and I — what the hell am I?"

"No, that's not why. I swear to God that's not the reason." Her eyes filled with tears at the thought of having hurt him.

"Wait. I want to show you something that'll make you understand."

Flora left the room, and returned a couple of minutes later, carrying a photo.

"Look at this."

Tony did as he was asked, but didn't understand why. It was an old school yearbook photo from about twenty years ago.

"I don't get it."

"That girl there is me and the boy next to me is Flavio. We were inseparable even then, sixteen years ago."

Tony nodded in silence, but even his silence pained her.

"Do you remember," she continued, "how desperate I was when I came to you for help to avenge the death of my man? I wouldn't be human if I were to forget him so quickly."

"That's true. But then there are things that happen against our wishes," he said, cryptically.

"I'm certain I would have been able to love you, had Flavio never existed."

"Love me?" A sneer twisted Tony's lips. "When would you ever have noticed someone like me if you hadn't needed a killer? Or should I say that it was your Flavio who brought us together. Do you believe in fate?"

Not knowing what to say, she looked pleadingly at him, but the young man turned and left the room without another word.

Once alone, she let the tears roll down her cheeks. She felt torn apart by pain, but it wasn't for Flavio's death, nor for the insult to his memory.

It was something new, something lethal, that had attacked her soul, but as yet she didn't know what it was.

* * *

They didn't speak much over the next few days,

but on the 26th May, on the eve of Tony's departure for Germany, Flora said something important.

"Tony, somebody follows me every time I leave home."

He looked shocked. "Do you know who it is?"

"No. They think they're being cunning by using a different car each time. First it was black, then white, then blue, but I always notice if there is a parked car that pulls away when I do. The driver wears a hat pulled down over his face, or a pair of dark glasses"

"The antiques dealer," murmured Tony. "He could have spoken to someone."

"Or what if there is a spy for the Mafia at the police station?" said Flora, "who told them what I said after the death those scum bags."

Tony shrugged. "Anything's possible in Sicily. But the driver's widow did say that she had seen a black man running away."

"A killer I paid for, which is what the police believe. Now how are we going to find out if Giancola is following you or me, or both of us?"

They were both silent for a minute, then Flora spoke.

"Wait a second. Even if people know that there is a man staying in my house, nobody knows who. The most plausible explanation would be that I'm living with my new lover, not with the killer I've paid. Actually, if they had thought that you were the man they were looking for, they would have broken in during the night and done away with you. You've changed the way you look, no one would recognise your face. My idea could still work."

"What idea?"

"That we show them that we are lovers. I'll come to Germany with you."

'How I wish you could,' thought Tony.

"I can't let you," he said instead, "I can't let you risk your life."

"I'll go straight back to the travel agents. Two return tickets for two lovers who are going to Lipsia to deliver a couple of paintings and who will then stay on for a week to see the city. Yes, that's what we'll do. We'll see the sights of Lipsia together. If they do follow us that far, we'll spot them immediately," decided Flora quickly.

Tony didn't dare say anything.

* * *

At eight o'clock the next morning, they were at the airport. After having checked the paintings in — perfectly packaged and in full view of all the passengers — they were left carrying a small bag each, perfect for a short trip away. In his, Tony had the two hundred euros, buried under a couple of shirts, two pairs of boxers and a two pairs of shirts. To the couple of pairs of panties Flora had packed for herself, she had added lots of other things for Tony she thought could come in handy, including medicine and a razor.

His gun however, was back at the villa as they would have never got through the metal detector. Who knows, maybe it was better that he didn't have it with him in Germany, that he passed himself off as a peaceful type who didn't carry a weapon. And anyway, should things get difficult, another weapon could always be found.

Once on plane, they looked around them suspiciously.

"Can you see anyone dodgy?" whispered Flora.

Tony shook his head.

"I'm pretty sure that if they are following us, they'll travel by car or train so that they can take their weapons with them."

They landed in Lipsia without incident, but even when they arrived at the hotel they continued to look around them suspiciously, like mice that sense the presence of a cat.

"Can you see anything?" asked Flora as Tony leaned out of the window.

"No."

"By now they'll have accepted that we aren't the people they're looking for. Why should they just follow the one lead?" she said, hopefully. "Giancola's got loads of enemies, and I'd imagine that there are plenty who are far more cunning than we are, wouldn't you?"

Tony agreed. "Now I've got to prove that I really am here to deliver the paintings, and that an ambush is the last thing on my mind," he said. "Give me Schmidt's number."

Flora gave him the business card.

"Does this guy understand Italian?" asked the young man, grabbing the phone off the bedside table.

"Enough."

Tony dialled the number. "Hello? Herr Schmidt? I'm the courier from Italy. I've got two paintings here from Signora Persici. Yes. Five o'clock this afternoon. Thank you." He put the telephone down and turned to Flora.

"I need to be there at five. I'll take a taxi."

Flora gave him a receipt from the art gallery.

"Give him this once he's given you twelve hundred euros."

* * *

By six o'clock he was back at the hotel unscathed, with 1200 euros in his pocket. He took off his false glasses and sat down with a sigh of relief.

"Did anyone follow you?" asked Flora.

"No," he replied, but he was lying, and since his eyes were incapable of hiding the truth, he turned away from her. Yes, a dark car had followed his taxi. And if the gangsters were already in Germany, it meant that they had found out from the travel agents where they were going, and had left Sicily in the car a couple of days before they did! He couldn't fault their powers of organisation. As they hadn't shot him yet, it could only mean that they were still unsure that he was the man they were looking for. They were obviously waiting for him to give himself away. But how?

"Good," said Flora. "While you were out, I completed our action plan. We're going to play the part of two happy lovers who have decided to spend a week seeing Lipsia, and then we are going to have the most enormous row.

We'll make sure everybody at the hotel hears us arguing, and then we'll go our separate ways. I'll go back to Italy, and you'll take the two hundred thousand euros and go wherever you please. If you want to work in Germany, you've got a week to decide what you're going to do."

"You're ever so good at organising the lives of others," commented Tony.

It pained her to have to talk to him this way, as if she were talking to a perfect stranger, but he had been so cold towards her lately that she felt as if she didn't have a choice.

"When we separate," she continued in the same neutral tone, "any spy would have to chose whom to follow. Will it be me or you? One of us will be free."

'There's no point,' thought Tony, 'I'm the one they're

after. I can't stay another week here, pretending that's everything's fine, pretending to be loved by a woman who doesn't love me.'

"I already know what I'll do," he said, "I'm going to become a poor immigrant in search of work as a shop boy."

"Are you mad!" shouted Flora. "You'll have two hundred thousand euros!"

"I don't want that money any more."

Flora was shocked. "What do you mean you don't want that money? It's yours. You could open a shop with it."

"No, I couldn't. Don't you understand that it would be impossible? Do you really believe that the German authorities will give a trading licence to the first stranger that knocks on their door? You artists live with your heads in the clouds! They would ask me for my birth certificate and other documents that I couldn't possibly give them because I've got a false identity card."

Flora thought about it for a moment. "But even if you are just a simple factory worker and not a shop owner, the two hundred thousand euros would make life a lot easier for you."

"I don't want the money. Give me ten thousand for a car and anything else I might need to start my new life here."

"I don't understand. I sold my house to give you that money."

"I'm sorry about the house, but I've changed my mind."

"Why?"

Tony stared out of the window without replying.

"You've earned that money," she insisted. "You can't go back to work for the Agostas, and that's my fault. You deserve to be compensated for all the trouble I've put you through."

Again, Tony didn't say anything. He turned away.

"Tony, look me in the eyes and tell me what's going on."

"Excuse me," he said, "I need to go to the bathroom."

He went into the bathroom and locked the door. Flora sat on the bed, gripped with a sense of unease that made her heartbeat quicken. 'What's the matter with Tony? What does he know that I don't?'

She did the only thing she could do and followed her instinct. She went up to the bathroom door, and started to talk.

"Tony, listen to me. Whatever you decide to do, I need you to know that I love you."

There was no reply. She continued, her voice breaking with emotion. "I know that you won't believe me. But nature is cruel beast. She lets me love someone for sixteen years, she convinces me that he is the only man who will ever make me happy and then….as quick as a flash, she deletes him from my soul. Why? I don't know. I could continue to cry every time I see a photo of Flavio, to get angry because he didn't deserve to die the way he did. I'll continue to suffer because a part of my life has been torn from me. But that doesn't mean that I have to push you away and devote myself to his memory. It's your eyes I want to look into now, it's your body that I want to feel on mine, and it's your soul that has become a part of mine because we think in the same way. It's your voice that soothes me when you talk about my paintings Tony! I love you; I know that now for sure. I have loved you since the day you arrived at my house, with your wounded shoulder and looked at me with the eyes of a hounded animal. Flavio's not here anymore, but you're alive. You're alive! Please don't hide yourself behind that door. I want you! Come out, damn it!"

She punched the door and waited. After a couple of minutes, the young man came out of the bathroom and looked at her, his large, sincere, eyes shining with tears.

"Say that you believe me!" implored Flora. "Say that —"

But Tony didn't let her continue. His lips pressed against hers, his arms lifted her up and carried her over to the bed and she surrendered herself to him.

They made love and did it with passion, but also with ease, as if they had always done it, as if they knew every millimetre of each other's body by heart. There was no need for words. When Flora realised that he was crying, she didn't ask him why, rather she turned and kissed his tears, murmuring: "We'll stay together."

"No. No we can't."

"Yes we can. You can't go home, and I don't have to. I've got no one waiting for me in Sicily. We'll stay in Germany; we've got loads of money, and as I'm not the one with fake documents, I'll open the shop. A shop that sells paintings, and I'll start painting again and we'll sell my work. What a lovely idea! And you can help me in the shop. As long as no one kills us, that is."

"No Flora, you can't stay with me. You're a law abiding citizen and I'm a killer and that's all there is to it."

"A law-abiding citizen?" She laughed. "I've hired two murderers and stabbed a homeless man. Do you really think that I'm better than you?"

"But you didn't do those things for money."

"It doesn't matter," said Flora. "I'm just like you. And anyway, your life as a killer is over. I'll teach you how to paint!"

"You're only saying that because you don't want me to see the huge abyss that separates us."

"There's no abyss, Tony. Don't leave me. I can't live without you. Bad memories stop me from painting."

He didn't promise her anything because he didn't know how to lie.

"Swear that you'll stay with me."

"I can't. I'll ruin your life. Do you remember what you said before? That maybe we'll discover that the spies will follow me and not you," replied Tony.

"When I said that, I thought you didn't love me. Everything's changed now. If someone wants to shoot you, I'd rather they shot me as well.

Tony felt the tears fill his eyes again.

"Hold me," was all he said. "Hold me tight."

* * *

They made love again after dinner, and Flora, exhausted by multiple orgasms, slept deeply. When she woke up, there was nobody in bed next to her.

"Tony?"

Silence. Flora got out of bed and opened the bathroom door, but he wasn't there either. Gripped by a sense of foreboding, she went over to where they had left their bags. Tony's bag was missing and the money was in her bag attached to a note.

Dear Flora,

I've taken 10,000 euros I needed, and by the time you read this, I'll be on the road heading towards Hamburg. Don't come looking for me. Enjoy Lipsia for another couple of days and when you're certain that nobody's following you, go back to Palermo.

If you are ever harassed by anyone, call this number: 3382459702. One of the Agostas will reply and you should ask them for protection. You'll have no problems paying them because I've left you one hundred and ninety thousand euros. That's all I can do for you.

I love you.

Tony.

"No!" screamed Flora. "No!" She knew his mobile phone number by heart. She dialled it immediately, but his phone was switched off.

That's normal, she thought. He'll be in a second-hand car showroom trying to get himself a good deal. He doesn't even speak German; it won't be easy for him.

But then she thought: 'Why should Tony turn his phone on? He won't want me to call him, and there's no one else who'll want to call him. He hasn't got any friends or relatives, or an employer. He'll leave his telephone off until he finds work. Oh God no! Please God, make him turn his phone on.'

* * *

Maybe Tony had a sixth sense, because at around ten o'clock he turned his phone on and put it on the passenger seat of his car. Almost immediately it rang, and although he feared that it would be painful, forced himself to answer.

"Hello?"

"Don't do it!" said a feminine voice, made unrecognisable by desperation. "Come back to me Tony! Come back to the hotel!"

He didn't have the courage to reply, but neither did he have the strength to end the call. He stayed on the line, listening to that beloved voice that both caressed and tormented his soul at the same time.

"Please!" said Flora. "Please, where do you want to go without any money? Why Hamburg? Can you hear me? Tony? Darling, come to me! Please come back to me! Please. I want to spend the rest of my life with you!"

He turned off his phone and blinked until the tears that were blurring his vision fell down his cheeks and he could see the road once more. But the road wasn't the only thing he had to keep an eye on. He was being followed by a dark car, driven by a young, thin man with the face of a rat.

Tony had already noticed the man outside Herr Schmidt's house when he was delivering the paintings. He had also recognised his face at the car dealership, and now was in no doubt that the bastard was after him. He couldn't run away forever.

He suddenly changed direction and turned into a road that led into open countryside, but he had no intention of trying to lose his shadow. When he was sure he had found an isolated spot, he stopped, forcing the other driver to stop too.

Tony got out of his car, took off his glasses, and walked towards his enemy, hoping to receive a bullet to the chest before he got to the other car. But rat face wasn't ready to lay his cards on the table quite yet and was pretending to talk on the telephone.

"Hey you!" said Tony, when he was close enough to be heard, "get out of the car."

With studied innocence, the other man put down his phone, and said:

"What do you want from me?"

"I know that you're following me. Do what you have to do; I'm not armed."

"I wasn't following you, for fuck's sake. I was making a call."

"Yeah right. What are the odds of me, a Sicilian, and you, a Sicilian, meeting in Germany like this? Come on then. Let's get this over with. I'm Tony Santarosa and in the past I worked for the Agosta family. Who do you work for? For Davide Giancola, or for his brother?"

On hearing the name of his boss, rat face put his hand in his jacket pocket and pulled out a gun.

"Now we're getting somewhere," said Tony. "I'm the one you're looking for. You haven't shot me yet because you weren't sure it was me, right? I'd like to know something before I die. Who put you on to me?"

"Uncle Cesare. But we were on the trail of another too, a forty something who had also asked him for fake documents," replied rat face.

"I see," said Tony, putting his hands up in surrender. "Wait a moment before shooting me, there's something I'd like you to tell the Giancola family."

"What?"

"Carlo and Saverio had fucked up. Without their boss knowing, they robbed couples and raped women. Sooner or later they would have got Giancola into a hell of a lot of trouble. I killed them because they raped my cousin. It was a personal vendetta. The Agostas don't know anything about what I did; they're innocent."

"And the seventeen year old?" asked rat face. "Why did you kill him?"

"Because he was in the wrong place at the wrong time. He was with Saverio, and when I shot Saverio, he shot me. His bullet glanced my shoulder. I was forced to kill him without knowing who he was."

The killer fiddled with his pistol. "I'll tell him," he said. "What was the painter's role in all this?"

"She's got nothing to do with it. She's my lover and she wanted me to leave Italy because she thought the police were looking for me. She knows nothing about the Mafia. Leave her alone. I brought you here so you wouldn't shoot me when I was with Flora."

Rat face smiled and snapped safety catch off.

"So she really was your lover!" he exclaimed. "Who would have thought? That woman was way out of your league."

"I know," said Tony. "She deserves better."

He closed his eyes and waited for the shot.

* * *

Flora heard the news on the TV. She didn't understand German, but the images spoke for themselves: first there was a photo of a man lying on the ground next to a main road, and then a photo. A photo of a fake identity card.

Her tears didn't take long to dry. They were replaced by a feeling of haziness that hits people who no longer feel attached to anything in this world. She didn't know that Tony had willingly gone to his death to save her, but she knew that she had been duped by fate that had killed the man she loved to avenge the death of a previous love.

What did she have left? Only the desire to join both of her lovers in the next world.

She didn't go down to lunch, but shut herself in her room at the hotel. She sent the cleaner away, and when, at four o'clock in the afternoon, somebody knocked at her door, she really did hope that it was 'her' killer. Someone sent to shoot her in the head.

Without hesitating, she opened the door and found herself staring at a delivery boy with a large bunch of chrysanthemums in his hand.

"Frau Persici?"

"Yes?"

"These are for you."The boy gave her the flowers and disappeared.

Great, thought Flora, are they poisoned, or will they explode in my hands? Instinctively she looked for a card, and found one.

We are sorry girl, but your boyfriend was a son of a bitch.

It wasn't signed.

That was all. A joke, a horrible joke. There was something missing from the card and she struggled to understand what it was.

You'll be next!

Yes, that was it. So...

"Didn't you know?" she said out loud, as though the Giancolas were able to hear her. "Didn't you know that it was me who hired Tony? That I was the one who commissioned the murders?"

She'd got away with it and she would never have known had those bastards not decided to taunt her with a bunch of chrysanthemums.

She started to laugh and laugh until she became hysterical and every laugh was followed by a sob.

* * *

Now, back in her villa in Palermo, she didn't know

where to start.

She had Tony's painting framed and hung in the living room, and then spent five days slumped on the sofa, drinking cherry brandy and staring at it. She wasn't used to alcohol and it didn't take long before she was drunk.

But on the sixth day she decided she couldn't carry on drinking herself to death. She had to do something.

She picked up her mobile phone and dialled the number that Tony had written in his farewell letter.

"Hello?" said a male voice.

"I'm Tony Santarosa's woman," replied Flora. "I need to see you."

"I don't know anyone called Tony, I'm afraid you've got the wrong number," said the man on the other end of the phone who was obviously intent on ending the conversation as quickly as possible.

"Wait, I'm one of yours. I was with Tony when he told you he was ill. He wasn't ill, he was leaving for Germany and he was killed there."

Maybe this information aroused the curiosity of the gangster, for he stayed on the line. She continued:

"Before he died, Tony gave me this number and told me that in case of emergency I could call you. I don't even know your name, but I've got a job for you and a lot of money to pay you with."

At the word 'money', the man's tone changed.

"I don't like talking about certain things on my mobile," he replied, "If you give me your number, I'll call you back from a phone booth."

"My name's Flora Persici and my home phone number's in the phone book."

"Are you mad? You should never give your real name over the telephone."

"Nobody's listening in to this call. Look me up in the phone book: Flora Persici."

The line went dead and she feared she had lost her only chance....was it really that bad telling someone your name over the phone?

But despite everything, five minutes later, the telephone rang.

The gangster's voice was slightly friendlier.

"I saw your address in the phone book, doll. Seems to me you live in a very nice area."

"I told you I wasn't from the police."

"How on earth did Tony manage to bag himself a woman like you? You're not one of those high class hookers are you?"

"No, I'm a painter. Where can we meet up?"

The man hesitated and then said:

"At five o'clock in the English Gardens. There's a bench under the largest magnolia tree."

"How will I recognise you?"

"I'll come to *you* honey. What do you look like?"

"I'm tall and blonde and thin. I'm thirty-one years old."

"I'll be there," and then the stranger put the phone down.

At five o'clock that afternoon, Flora was sat on the bench under the magnolia tree but it wasn't until a quarter past five that the man came and sat down next to her. He was dark haired and his skin, which was also dark, had shrivelled under the sun; as to his age, she would have guessed anywhere between forty-five and sixty.

"Sorry I'm late," he whispered, "I wanted to check that there weren't any police in the park."

She smiled. "And what about those in plain clothes?"

"Those are easy to spot. They're the ones pretending

to read the newspaper. No, there are only mothers and babies and pensioners with dogs here today. So what do you want?"

"A paid favour. I want to know which of Giancola's men has been to Germany recently. Around the twenty-sixth and the twenty-eighth of May."

"Okay, I could get that information for you. What else?"

"He killed Tony. I want him dead. Clipped. Taken out."

The gangster shook his head. "No honey. I won't be killing one of Giancola's men. He'd have one of *ours* killed the next week."

"I know, but it doesn't have to look like a Mafia hit. You could hire a couple of down and outs and pretend it was a robbery. It would be even better if there was also a woman on the scene, a foreign prostitute might work. The newspapers will report that the man was robbed by a couple of tramps; no one would guess it was a member of the Agosta family."

"It'll cost you a pretty penny, paying for all these people."

"You've lost Tony, who worked for you. Sooner or later you'll replace him with another Sicilian and no one will connect the story of the tramps and the robbery with his death. I can pay you thirty thousand euros."

The stranger looked at her and smiled mockingly.

"Who are you? A criminal mastermind?"

"Quite possibly. Tony once said the same thing to me."

"Why do you want to spend all this money?"

"Because in Germany that son of a bitch killed the man I loved."

The gangster seemed convinced. "Thirty thousand for the tramps, and ten thousand to me for the commission," he said. "That forty thousand all in."

She agreed. "Twenty thousand as a down payment," she replied and without hesitating, opened her bag and showed him the contents. The gangster stared at the money greedily.

"Can I do any other favours for you?"

"One thing at a time. I would like to get Davide Giancola locked up, because I know that none of you would dare kill him. If you could point me in the direction of someone who would be willing to collect evidence of his illegal activities. A couple of photos, a bit of wire tapping, the kind of thing the cops love. He will be well paid and won't be at risk from retribution because I'll be the one who'll take the evidence to the police. I'll do everything and afterwards I'll ask to be admitted into the witness protection program. I'll end up living in a quaint village up north in Piedmont or Aosta."

"You're out of your mind. None of Giancola's henchmen would sell him out for twenty thousand shitty euros."

"But for one hundred and fifty thousand euros," replied Flora, having calculated what she would have left after paying for the first murder, "someone just might. It may not seem like a lot of money to a 'made man' in the Giancola family, but for a simple stooge — like the new driver — it just might be enough."

"A hundred fifty thousand euros?" stuttered the gangster.

"Yes. I'll get the boss sent down and I'll be the only one risking their life to do so. I'll also be doing a favour to the Agosta family, won't I? Because if Giancola's off the scene, then this patch is all yours."

It had always been the dream of the Agosta family to get rid of the Giancolas, but to do so would have meant risking the life of the whole 'family', which no one had had the guts to do. No one that is, until now. Here she was, this blonde woman, this perfect stranger, was offering to risk her life for the family and seemed as indifferent as a kamikaze pilot who was about to blow himself up to destroy an enemy.

"Who are you, really?" asked the man from the Agostas.

"A painter. But that doesn't matter. Now I'm one of yours."

'No,' said Tony's shadow, 'don't do it. I died trying to keep you out of all this. I died wishing that I'd never killed anybody, that I was an honest father with a family, to see my mother again and to introduce her to our child. Don't do it Flora. Don't avenge my death, I beg you."

But shadows have silent voices and Flora couldn't hear him.